“In r [illegible]
man [illegible] they’re bonded for life.”

“Hang on.” Cody planted his feet in the loamy soil. “Is that what you’re after, Faith? A lifetime bond?”

“No, silly. I already told you this is a temporary deal. We each have our lives set up the way we want them so why mess with that?”

He continued to study her. “But what if you find out you really like it?”

“I hope to Hannah I’ll like it. This is my only shot so I want it to be good.”

“That’s my point. What if it’s so freaking wonderful that you want to keep doing it for longer than two weeks?”

“I doubt that.”

For some reason, he found that funny. “How can you be so sure?”

“Easy. Judging from all the books I’ve read, it’s exciting the first few times, but then the story has to end because after that it gets boring. It’s just wash, rinse, repeat.”

A COWBOY'S HONOR

THE MCGAVIN BROTHERS

Vicki Lewis Thompson

Ocean Dance Press

A COWBOY'S HONOR

ISBN: 978-1-946759-14-6

Ocean Dance Press LLC
PO Box 69901
Oro Valley, AZ 85737

Cover art by Kristin Bryant

Visit the author's website at
VickiLewisThompson.com

Want more cowboys? Check out these other titles by Vicki Lewis Thompson

The McGavin Brothers

A Cowboy's Strength
A Cowboy's Honor
A Cowboy's Return

Thunder Mountain Brotherhood

Midnight Thunder
Thunderstruck
Rolling Like Thunder
A Cowboy Under the Mistletoe
Cowboy All Night
Cowboy After Dark
Cowboy Untamed
Cowboy Unwrapped
In the Cowboy's Arms
Say Yes to the Cowboy
Do You Take This Cowboy?

Sons of Chance

Wanted!
Ambushed!
Claimed!
Should've Been a Cowboy
Cowboy Up
Cowboys Like Us
Long Road Home
Lead Me Home
Feels Like Home
I Cross My Heart

Wild at Heart
The Heart Won't Lie
Cowboys and Angels
Riding High
Riding Hard
Riding Home
A Last Chance Christmas

1

Cody McGavin's heart always lifted with his first glimpse of the single-story, rambling log house that was the heart of Wild Creek Ranch. Home. The place looked about the same as it had when he'd left two months ago except the snow had melted off the roof and someone had planted daisies in the flower beds.

He glanced at the forest green truck parked beside the house. Their new hire, Faith Underwood, must be having trouble with her vintage F150. The driver's door was open and she lay on her back on the floorboard fooling with something under the dash.

Cody pulled in beside her and cut the engine. Although she was a better mechanic than he was, a true cowboy always offered to help a woman having trouble with her vehicle.

And Faith was a woman, although when he and his brother Zane had first laid eyes on her two months ago, neither of them had been sure. Her old boots, baggy jeans, loose plaid shirt and roomy vest hadn't given them a clue about her gender. She'd tucked her hair up under her hat, too. Until they'd seen her delicate features and had heard her voice, they'd been guessing.

She wore a similar outfit today, minus the vest since Montana's June sunshine had warmed things up considerably. In the time since she'd been hired, Zane had reported that she was a good hand down at the stable and invaluable to their mom, who'd been laid up with a broken leg. Cody hadn't been much help on that deal because he'd had to go back to his job at the Triangle V.

Shutting off the engine, he climbed out of his truck and walked around the back of hers. "Hey, Faith, what's going on?"

She squirmed out from under the dash and stood. She looked a little more like a girl today without her hat, which she'd hung on the truck's antenna while she worked. She'd put her hair in a single braid and the late afternoon sun picked out some red in it, although she was mostly blond. She shaded her eyes with her hand. "Hey, Cody. You're back."

"For a little while, anyway. Can I help you with something?"

"You surely could if it's not too much of an imposition." She held up the part she'd taken out from under the dash. "Starter. I knew it was going, even bought a new one, but I never got around to installing it. If you could run me home tonight and fetch me again in the morning, I'll just leave the truck here for now and fix it tomorrow."

"I'd be happy to." Considering the glowing praise Zane had heaped on Faith's performance, it was the least he could do. "Just let me pop inside, say hi to Mom and tell her where I'm going."

"Okay." Faith gave him a big smile. "She made your favorite dinner."

"I thought I smelled pot roast." He'd forgotten that Faith had a little gap between her two front teeth. She didn't wear makeup, so between her freckles and her gap-toothed smile, she looked more like a kid than a grown woman. "See you in a few." Tapping two fingers on the brim of his hat, he turned and walked quickly up the flagstone path to the front porch. The aroma of a simmering roast grew stronger when he opened the front door. He looked forward to eating his mom's cooking for the next couple of weeks.

She came out of the kitchen, moving awkwardly on her walking cast, but her face was flushed with happiness. "You're here!"

"Hey, Mom." He crossed to her and gathered her in his arms. The top of her head only reached to his chin and he rested his cheek on her dark hair as he gave her a tight hug. Then he stepped back and looked down at the cast sticking out of her baggy sweats. She'd painted her toenails royal purple. "How's your leg?"

"Driving me crazy, but at least I got rid of the stupid crutches and the dumb wheelchair."

"I wondered how long you'd tolerate a wheelchair."

"About three days." Her eyes sparkled as she gazed up at him. "Come on in the kitchen. Dinner won't be for a while yet but I'll get you a snack."

"Sounds good, but first I need to run Faith home. The starter went out on her truck."

She frowned. "That's a bummer. Everything in Eagles Nest is closed by now."

"It's okay. She was anticipating it and so she has a new one at home. I'll pick her up in the morning and she'll be all set." He backed toward the door. "I won't be long."

"Good. I want to hear the latest plans for your trip. Zane and Mandy are coming for dinner. Jo is, too, and she's bringing chocolate cake."

"Excellent." His mom's pot roast and Aunt Jo's chocolate cake. Life didn't get much better.

"We all want to know if you've decided on your route."

"More or less. Can't wait to see everybody." Giving her a quick tip of his hat, he headed out. He was glad that Zane, Mandy and Aunt Jo were coming to dinner. Aunt Jo was Mandy's mom and he and his brothers called her Aunt Jo because she'd been like a second mother. Mandy called their mom Aunt Kendra for the same reason.

Faith stood by his truck, her backpack over one shoulder and her hat tugged down so it shadowed her eyes. He couldn't remember what color they were. Not that it mattered. She was a mystery to him—a woman who acted like one of the guys, never flirted or giggled and didn't seem to care whether her clothes flattered her, which they most certainly didn't. He'd never met anyone like her.

But she was still female, so he walked to the passenger door and opened it for her because that was how he'd been raised.

"Thanks." She hopped in so quickly he didn't have time to offer a hand up.

"Welcome." He closed the door and rounded the front of his truck. The midnight blue paint job was almost as bad as black for showing dust and he might wash it tomorrow. But he'd have to get used to a dirty truck when he took his road trip, so maybe he'd leave it this way. He couldn't waste precious time keeping his vehicle spiffy once he began his adventure.

Climbing behind the wheel, he made sure Faith was buckled up before he backed out of the parking space and started down the ranch road that led to the paved two-lane into town. "I have a general idea where you live," he said, "but you'd better give me directions."

"Sure. Drive into Eagles Nest and take a left at Rawhide. We're on a little dirt road on the outskirts of town. I'll tell you when to turn."

"Is it Wagon Wheel Lane?"

"That's it."

"Then I know exactly where I'm going." He used to date someone on Wagon Wheel Lane but he decided not to bring that up.

"We only have a little over two acres, but it works for us."

"Am I right that you live with your dad?" Now that he had a chance to talk one-on-one, he might as well find out more about this puzzling woman. She looked like a teenager but was probably older, like in her mid-twenties, basically the same age as him.

"I do. He's semi-retired."

"Really?" He thought of his mom, only forty-four and not even thinking about retirement. Maybe this guy had been much older when Faith was born.

"A horse rolled on him last year."

Cody winced. "That's not good."

"I know. All those weeks in the hospital took the spunk right out of him. The doctors say he's healed but he says he's never getting on a horse again. I can't imagine that, but his choice, right?"

"Guess so." He reached the paved road and turned left into town.

"But I don't want to talk about my dad. I have a confession to make."

Now there was a comment he hadn't expected. He glanced over at her as a trickle of uneasiness ran down his spine. "Like what?"

"There's nothing wrong with my starter. I left it on the floor of the truck and I'll just reinstall it tomorrow."

Oh, boy. He'd seen movies like this, where an apparently sane person was suddenly revealed to be a whack-a-doodle. "Uh, so why did you do that?"

"Because I wanted to talk with you privately."

There was only one possible reason for that and it scared him spitless. "Is it Mom? Is there something nobody's telling me about her condition?"

"Heavens, no! Kendra's doing great. She's amazing."

He let out a breath and relaxed. "Okay, so not Mom."

"No. It's more personal."

His uneasiness returned. He was very glad they were approaching the Eagles Nest town limits. If necessary, he'd turn in somewhere, like the diner parking lot, so he could give her his complete attention. "But I don't really know you. Why would you want to discuss something personal with me?"

"Because it also involves you."

"How can that be? This is the longest conversation you and I have ever had." And the weirdest one.

She sighed. "This seemed so logical when I came up with it but now I'm afraid you'll think I'm nuts."

Too late.

"But the timing is so perfect. You'll be at the ranch for about two weeks, right?"

"That all depends." *On whether you're crazy and I need to get far, far away from you.*

"Look, I've talked to your mom and I know you haven't figured out what you're doing about a horse for your trip."

"I'll come up with something." His grand plan, to spend two months videotaping remote wilderness areas of the West on horseback, required a horse trailer and a horse. The trailer wasn't a big deal. He could buy one and sell it later. A horse—not so much. He couldn't in good conscience take one of the horses that Wild Creek Ranch needed for trail rides. He could buy a horse and then sell it to the ranch, but they didn't have room for another one right now.

"I want to loan you my horse."

"Oh. I didn't know you had one."

"My dad and I each have a horse, although he never rides Ernie so I'm doing my best to keep both Ernie and Bert exercised. I don't always get that accomplished, though."

"So that's what this private talk is all about? Me borrowing your horse so he can get some exercise?" If so, that would be great, but he couldn't understand her need for privacy.

"That's only part of it."

"Listen, if you want me to pay you for taking Bert, I'm fine with that. I thought about renting a horse but this would be way better. Zane says you're a first-rate trainer so I'd know what I'd be getting."

"I'm not looking for any payment but I do have a big favor to ask."

Uh-oh. Here came the catch. "What's that?"

"See, the thing is, I'm a virgin."

He flipped on his signal and pulled into the diner parking lot.

"Why did you turn in here?"

Switching off the engine, he glanced at her and swallowed. "Because the conversation is getting very strange and I don't want to have a wreck."

"I shouldn't have blurted it out. I've been told I'm blunt."

And looney tunes. Had anyone told her that? "I can't begin to imagine what your virginity has to do with loaning me a horse so you'll have to make that connection. My mind boggles."

"It's simple." She unfastened her seatbelt so she could turn to face him. "You're the most beautiful man I've ever laid eyes on."

Yep, completely bonkers. He couldn't imagine how his mom and Zane had missed that pertinent fact. "I don't know about—"

"Come on, Cody. Everybody agrees—your mom, Zane, Mandy, Jo—you're considered the prettiest of the bunch."

"Guys don't like being called pretty." But he had been. She wasn't wrong about the way his family carried on about his looks.

"Okay, then—handsome! In any case, I see your two-week visit as a gift from the heavens. I would like to be deflowered, and I can't think of anyone I'd rather have do the deed than you."

His brain whirled. "Who says *deflowered* these days?"

"I do. It's a cool word. Are you in? My horse in exchange for a deflowering?"

"Faith, you're not making any sense. We don't even know each other."

"I'll admit that you don't know me, but I've learned a fair amount about you. They say you're a little spoiled, but—"

"Hey, I'm *not* spoiled."

"You're the baby of the family. It goes with the territory. But they said a *little* spoiled. Nobody described you as a tyrant who demands to get his way all the time. The main thing is that everyone I've talked to says you can be trusted. That's important to me. If we do this thing, I don't want anyone to find out. It'll be our little secret."

"We're not doing it. I can't believe we're sitting in the parking lot of the Eagles Nest Diner discussing this like it's a business deal."

"It's a deal, but it's not about business." She held his gaze. "Give yourself a chance to think about it before you reject the idea."

Green. Her eyes were green. And judging from the way they glowed with anticipation, she was dead serious about this outrageous proposition. He was rarely at a loss for words but this time he was speechless.

"I've freaked you out."

He nodded.

"I can understand that. I've been thinking about this for two months so I'm used to the idea, but—"

"*Two months*?" He sounded hoarse.

"Ever since the day I was hired, but I thought it was an impossible fantasy. Then Kendra mentioned that you'd be home for a couple of weeks to prepare for your big trip. When I found out that you weren't sure what to do about a horse, everything fell into place."

He cleared his throat. Time to put an end to this nonsense. "Listen, I'm flattered, very flattered and honored, but—"

"Like I said, don't decide right now." She said it quickly, nervously. Her eyes had lost their eager glow and her expression had grown tense. This obviously meant a lot to her. "I don't need an answer this very minute."

Damn. He hated lose-lose situations with a passion and this was shaping up to be one. She might be a great mechanic and a hell of a horsewoman, but when it came to male-female relationships, she was an innocent. Literally an innocent.

She wasn't crazy, but she seemed that way because she was incredibly naïve. If he rejected her request, she'd be hurt. Maybe even devastated. But if he took on the challenge...he could mess up six ways to Sunday. He'd only had one experience with a virgin and he'd been one at the time, too. That encounter had been a complete disaster, but a puppy love attraction had gotten them through it.

He wasn't even slightly in love with Faith. She might have a crush on him, but it was probably the kind that teenage girls have for a guy in a boy band. Guaranteed she'd have unrealistic expectations he'd never come close to fulfilling.

She buckled her seatbelt and the click sounded very loud in the complete silence of the cab. "Listen, I know you want to get back so you can have dinner with your family, and my dad's expecting me home, so we should get going."

"Right." He reached for the key and started the truck.

"I won't keep you there long, but I need to introduce you to my horse, Bert, so you can see what a sweetheart he is. And you can meet my dad, too."

Oh, like *that* wouldn't be awkward as hell. Cody began to sweat.

2

Faith had counted on the prospect of deflowering a virgin to excite Cody enough that he'd agree on the spot. Instead he'd looked worried about it. That wasn't the usual reaction of the heroes in the stories she'd been reading for a solid year.

The paperbacks had belonged to the wife of the ranch owner she and her dad had been working for when the accident had happened. Mrs. Preston had offered the books to occupy Faith's time while she hung out at the hospital during her dad's many operations. Most of the stories had been set in olden times, so perhaps modern men didn't have the same thoughts about virgins. Come to think of it, the modern stories hadn't had any virgins in them at all.

She'd shocked Cody so bad that he didn't talk the rest of the way to her house. But at least he hadn't refused her yet. She'd gathered from the scenes in her books that men were enthusiastic about sex, so if Cody gave himself time, he might see the advantage in this setup.

Then she had another thought that could louse up her plan. "Did you just get a girlfriend?"

"No." He turned down Wagon Wheel Lane.

"That's a relief. I've listened real close whenever Kendra talks about you and it sounded like you don't have one. But if you do, then I take back my request. I would never ask you to betray a steady girlfriend. You can still borrow my horse, though."

"I've discovered that a steady girlfriend is a tricky proposition when I'm working at the guest ranch. The single ladies who stay there like to flirt and they have more fun doing that if they know I'm unattached."

"But you could lie about it."

"Not my style."

She liked that answer and it fit what she'd heard about him so far. "So you haven't had a girlfriend in a while, then?"

"That's right."

"How long?" A dry spell could work to her advantage.

"I guess it's been about ten months."

"Well, there you go."

He glanced at her. "What?"

"You can relieve your frustrations with me and still not have a girlfriend when you go back to your job at the guest ranch. I could be the temporary answer to your prayers." She noticed a little dent in his cheek that told her he was either grimacing or trying not to smile.

"How much farther?"

"It's right up ahead. Turn at the yellow mailbox." The dirt road leading to the two-story frame house wasn't long. In no time she saw her dad's lanky frame in a rocker on the front porch.

Now that the weather was warmer he was usually there waiting for her.

Looked like he was repairing a bridle. He'd developed a reputation for fixing worn or frayed tack when they'd lived at the ranch and now folks who needed that service mailed it to him. Mostly it was small things like reins, girths and halters, but every so often someone shipped him a saddle. The work gave him something to do and brought in extra money.

"Where should I park?"

"Pull up in front. The yard's just dirt right now so you can't hurt anything. Dad and I are planning to lay down some gravel this summer and make a circular drive with a planter in the middle." She unlatched her seatbelt when the truck stopped. "I'll introduce you to my dad first and then we'll walk around to the barn. It's like a baby barn compared to the one at Wild Creek Ranch, but we only have two horses, so it's fine." She hopped down and started toward the porch.

Her dad laid aside the bridle and rose from his rocker. "Where's your truck, honey bun?"

"It was acting up so Cody gave me a ride home. I'll take care of the problem tomorrow." She turned around as Cody swung down and came toward them with his long-legged stride.

What a fine-looking cowboy. No wonder the guest ranch ladies enjoyed flirting with him. She swept an arm in his direction. "Dad, I'd like you to meet Cody McGavin. He's the youngest of the McGavin brothers. Cody, this is my father, Jim."

Cody climbed the steps and shook her dad's outstretched hand. "Pleased to meet you, Mr. Underwood."

"Same here, and call me Jim. Thanks for bringing my girl home."

"My pleasure. She's done a lot for my mom."

"I heard about your mom's leg. How's she doing?"

"Well, thank goodness. Faith said you took a bad spill a while back."

"Yep." Her dad rubbed his neck. "That was enough for me. I'm outta that game." He glanced at Cody. "Care to sit a while? I can offer you a beer."

"Thanks, but I need to take a rain check."

"Kendra's waiting dinner so Cody needs to get back to the ranch." Faith was touched that her dad had extended the hospitality and wished Cody could stay. Her dad didn't get out much and hadn't made any friends yet. "But first I want to take him down to meet Bert. I may be loaning out my horse for a little while."

"Oh?" Her dad looked surprised. "Why's that?"

"Long story. I'll explain later." She motioned to Cody. "Follow me around back."

"I fed them already," her dad called after her. "So don't let them tell you any different."

"I won't." She walked with Cody around the house to the small barn and the adjacent corral. She was proud of their tiny spread. For the first time in their lives, she and her dad owned property.

"This is nice." Cody glanced around. "Who takes care of everything?"

"Dad and I share the work. He does the cooking and cleans the inside of the house, plus makes sure the horses are fed and watered. I maintain the barn and the corral. Later this summer we might do some painting."

He glanced at her. "You sound excited about that."

"I am excited. Until two months ago, all I'd ever painted were houses and barns that belonged to someone else. I hate that Dad had the accident, but he got an insurance settlement and the silver lining is this place."

"Where were you before?"

"We'd worked on a ranch down near Billings for sixteen years. But I wanted to get Dad away from the bad memories so I looked for a small town close to the mountains with ranches in the area so I could find a job. Eagles Nest is perfect." She took note of where the sun was in the sky. "You need to get moving. Let's go see Bert and Ernie so you can be on your way."

The double doors into the barn worked smoothly because she'd seen to it. She rolled them back and stepped inside. "When I walked into this efficient little barn with only two stalls and a cubicle just big enough for our tack, I knew this was our spot. The house is perfect, too. I've always wanted to live in a two story and sleep upstairs. I have the whole top floor because Dad wanted the downstairs bedroom."

"I'm happy for you, Faith." His voice was filled with warmth for the first time. Not just friendliness, but actual emotional warmth.

She looked over her shoulder where he stood silhouetted in the doorway and wished the light were different so she could see his face. "Thank you."

Both horses poked their heads out of their stalls and Bert, who was in the first one, made a throaty little noise that was his typical greeting.

Faith walked over and rubbed the white blaze that ran from his forelock to the tip of his nose. "This is Bert."

Cody came to stand beside her. "I had a feeling, since his name's on the door."

"I had to do that."

"Because otherwise they couldn't remember where they belonged?"

"Exactly. They were forever hopping into the wrong stall."

"I figured that was it." He gave her a quick smile before stepping closer and stroking Bert's glossy neck. "Hey, Bert. How's it going, buddy?"

She'd had enough light to see that amazing smile before he turned away. If he accepted her proposition, then she'd find out what his mouth felt like when he kissed her. She'd fantasized about that a fair amount. She'd been kissed once before and she'd liked it until the encounter had turned ugly. Nothing involving Cody could ever turn ugly.

He would touch her, too, maybe stroke her body the way he was stroking Bert's chestnut coat. Little squiggly sensations traveled down her arms and legs. "Obviously, the bay is Ernie, and you should probably pet him, too, or he'll get jealous."

"Can't have that." With a final pat, Cody moved away from Bert's stall and transferred his attentions to Ernie.

Faith was a little shaky, which was probably an adrenaline rush. She folded her arms and took a deep breath. "So what do you think? Would Bert work for you?"

"He's a fine horse. I'd have to see if my saddle fits but I'm guessing it would. I'd want to ride him a little to make sure we get along."

"You'll get along. I've known Bert since he was a colt. You won't find a sweeter ride."

Cody turned toward her. "Wouldn't he miss you and Ernie?"

"Yes, but this would do him so much good and he'd have you with him twenty-four seven." She swallowed a lump of nervousness. "Now that you've seen him and you've had a chance to roll the idea around in your mind, what do you say?"

He gave Ernie a last scratch and walked back toward her. "Faith, giving a man your virginity should be something special."

Her heart hammered. "That's why I want to give it to you."

"I don't deserve to take that gift. Since you've waited this long, why not hold off until you find the man who'll share your life?"

"That's...that's not the way I see things working out."

"Why not?"

"I'm just not the type. Besides, my dad and I have a home now. We're settling in and it's enough for me." She hesitated. "But I want to know what it's like."

"Meaning..."

"Sex."

"Oh."

"Someone gave me a box of books last year and what happens in those books sounds nice. Fun, even." She gazed up at him. "I know you could show me and you'd be kind to a beginner."

He studied her intently for several seconds. "What if I'm not all you want me to be?"

"I'm not worried about that."

"I sure as hell am." He flinched. "Sorry. That kind of language doesn't belong in a discussion about lovemaking."

Despite the tension, she couldn't help but laugh. "I've lived and worked alongside trail-hardened cowboys all my life. A swear word now and then doesn't faze me. I've used them plenty of times myself."

"Maybe so, but I'd bet my hand-tooled saddle that you've never discussed this particular topic with those cowhands. And if you ever did, they wouldn't be using any swear words."

"That could be true."

"Look, I know you want an answer and I don't blame you. But I need to think about this. If you're willing to wait until tomorrow morning when I pick you up, I promise to decide one way or another by then."

She didn't have much choice. If she pushed him now, he'd probably turn her down. He still might, but maybe some time alone to imagine the possibilities would nudge him over to her way of thinking.

"Okay." She moved a step closer so they were almost touching. "But in case you decide the answer is no, would you be willing to kiss me right now? Then at least I'll have that."

He regarded her silently. She thought he would refuse, but then he took off his hat and hooked it on a vacant peg on the wall. He did the same with hers. Her heart beat so loud she was afraid he could hear it.

Moving closer, he framed her face in his big hands and tilted it up. "Close your eyes."

She squeezed them tightly shut.

"Not that much." There was a smile in his voice as he brushed his mouth over her eyelids. "Just normal closing, like you're going to sleep."

She relaxed her eye muscles. "How's that?"

"Better." He pressed his mouth to her forehead and feathered a light kiss over her cheekbones.

She wanted to ask him to do that again. It felt delicious. But he had to get home to his pot roast dinner. She also wanted to put her hands on his chest, but maybe he wouldn't like that, so she kept them at her sides.

"Now lick your lips."

She swept her tongue over her mouth. She thought he sucked in a breath but she might have been mistaken.

His breath warmed her mouth, tickling a little. "Leave your mouth open just a little bit. That's perfect. Now hold still." He gently touched his lips to hers. Moving slightly, he adjusted the fit and put a little more pressure on her mouth.

Oh, yes. This was lovely. The velvety texture and the subtle movement of his lips against hers made her dizzy. She wondered if she'd pass out from happiness.

Then he pulled back. "Breathe, Faith."

She opened her eyes.

"You're holding your breath, aren't you?"

She nodded.

"Well, stop it."

With a quick gasp, she drew in a lungful of air. "You're...supposed to breathe...when you kiss somebody?"

"Yes, ma'am." There was that dent in his cheek again.

This time she knew he was trying not to smile. "How does that work, kissing and breathing?"

"It just does." His chest was rising and falling darned fast, almost like he was excited.

That would be great if he was excited about kissing her. She wanted to try it again now that she knew about the breathing thing, but she couldn't justify keeping him here any longer. She'd promised the visit would be quick. "I'll remember that for next time." There might not be a next time but she'd think positive and assume she'd get another chance. "You need to get going."

"Yes, I do." He plucked his hat from the wall and handed hers over. "I'll be here at seven in the morning."

"I'll be ready." She walked him to his truck.

He called out a farewell to her dad, who was still on the porch, then settled behind the wheel. He tapped his fingers against the brim of his hat before starting the truck and driving away.

"Seems like a nice guy," her dad said from the porch.

"He is." She went up the steps and sat in the rocker that had been designated as hers. The porch had a good view of the mountains and the sunset. Now that the weather was nice, she and her dad had formed a habit of sitting outside to watch it. "His mom and brother are terrific, too."

"So what's this about loaning him Bert?"

She was prepared with half the story. "In a couple of weeks he's leaving for a two-month exploration of wilderness areas in the mountain ranges between here and Mexico and he needs a horse."

"I thought Wild Creek Ranch had a stable."

"It does, but all the horses are used for trail rides every weekend. Cody can't take one and leave them short. But he hesitated to get another one because the stable is full and he wouldn't have a place to keep it when he finishes his trip."

Her dad nodded. "I can see why Bert would be a good option, then." He'd abandoned the Stetson he used to wear for a baseball cap. She thought he looked better in the Stetson, but he'd stored it in his closet as if trappings like that didn't fit his new life.

"He could use the exercise, that's for sure. While Cody has him, I can ride Ernie more often."

"I can't decide what to do about that horse." He sighed and leaned back in his rocker. "I really should find him a new home."

"Don't do it yet. I'll need Ernie to ride while Bert's gone." She thought once her dad sold Ernie, his cowboy days would be over for good. Despite what he'd been through after the accident, she hated to see him give up riding completely. He used to love it and he'd passed on that love to her. She'd secretly hoped that once they were settled in this house she'd be able to coax him out for short rides, just the two of them. So far he'd refused.

"You don't have to twist my arm. I'm happy to procrastinate on that situation. Saying goodbye to Ernie will be very tough, but it's not fair to him that I'm holding on. He should be with someone who takes him out regularly."

"Like I said, I have a temporary solution for a couple of months. Then we can revisit the issue."

He glanced at her. "Meaning I might change my mind about riding?"

"Who knows?"

"I do. I won't change my mind." His tone indicated the subject was closed.

No point in challenging that kind of statement. Her dad was a stubborn man and prodding him when he'd taken a stand wouldn't yield results. Cody wasn't stubborn, though. He was just reluctant. She might need to be more seductive if she wanted him to agree with her plan.

Most of the heroines in the books were naturally seductive. All they had to do was sashay across a room or send a sidelong glance the hero's way and he was a puddle of lust. She had no idea how she could influence this decision in her favor, especially if Cody showed up in the morning with rejection on his mind.

At the moment, she had only one source of info on modern day thinking. She turned to her dad. "What first attracted you to Mom?"

He smiled. "That's an easy one. She smelled great."

Smelled great? What a strange answer. "Was it soap? Shampoo? Perfume?" If it was perfume, she was screwed. She didn't possess a single drop of the stuff.

"I don't know what it was, but she smelled like cookies baking. And you know how I love cookies."

That gave her a partial solution because most men loved cookies. She knew how to bake them and she had the ingredients, but she couldn't stuff cookies in her bra tomorrow morning. Wait a minute. She had an idea. It was worth a shot and desperate times called for desperate measures.

3

Enjoying pot roast with the family around the massive table in the dining room at Wild Creek Ranch had been big fun. Cody had missed being home. Things could change so fast, like Zane getting engaged to Mandy. She'd been Zane's good friend since they were three but they'd lost touch after high school when Mandy went off to be a fashion designer in New York.

They were certainly in touch, now. Mandy had moved back and was telecommuting with the New York office. Zane had never looked happier or more excited about the future. It was heartwarming to see how much he and Mandy loved each other.

Aunt Jo had to be over the moon about this new development. She and Mandy had lived on property adjoining McGavin land for years and the bond between the two families was strong.

Recently Aunt Jo had sold her house and land to Zane and moved to a condo in town. During dinner, she'd raved about maintenance-free condo living. Meanwhile, thanks to several generous donors, Zane would soon have a new and improved facility for his raptor rehabilitation project. He'd chosen a location within walking distance of the house that was surrounded by sheltering pines. He and Mandy hadn't set a date for their wedding, but it would be after Ryker, his and Zane's oldest brother, came home from his last tour of duty.

The June night was so balmy that everyone voted to have coffee and a piece of Aunt Jo's chocolate cake out on the porch. Faith's truck was still sitting in the front yard, so eventually Zane asked what the problem was.

"Starter went out." Cody was grateful for the dim lighting because he was a lousy liar.

"Huh." Zane blew across the top of his coffee to cool it. "I could've sworn she replaced that starter a month ago."

"Maybe she got a faulty starter." This story could unravel fast.

Sure enough, his mom spoke up. "Didn't you say she'd been expecting it to go and had a new one at home?"

"I might have misunderstood. My mind was occupied with thoughts about pot roast."

"Understandable," Zane said. "That was a fine meal, Mom. Thank you."

"You're welcome, but Faith deserves some of the credit. She helped me fix it."

"I met her dad today." Might as well keep the topic going because now that it had been broached, he was occupied with the subject of Faith and her outrageous proposition. "Have any of you met him?"

"I think you're the first," his mom said. "What's he like?"

"Friendly. Invited me for a beer, although I didn't take him up on it. His name's Jim. They have a nice place out there on Wagon Wheel Lane. Small, but well kept. Cozy, in a way." He hesitated. "Faith offered to loan me her horse for my trip."

Zane shot him a look. "You mean Bert?"

"So you know about Bert?"

"Yep. She's mentioned that she and her dad each have a horse, although her dad doesn't ride anymore. That's generous, bro, loaning you her horse for two months."

No kidding. "She said he and Ernie don't get enough exercise, so if I take Bert on my trip, she can spend more time with Ernie."

Mandy started giggling. "I'm sorry, Cody, but I can't keep hearing Bert and Ernie without thinking of those two characters on Sesame Street."

"The names sort of fit. Bert's a little taller and Ernie's on the chunky side."

"Faith must have watched the show," Aunt Jo said.

"Didn't we all." Mandy glanced fondly at Zane. "But it's hard to imagine Faith sitting in front of a TV. Aunt Kendra, didn't you say she lived in the bunkhouse with the cowhands when she was a kid?"

"Yes, and she loved it. Unfortunately, when she went to school she couldn't relate to the girls but the boys didn't accept her, either."

Cody's chest grew tight. Poor Faith, not fitting into either world. He couldn't get that kiss out of his mind, either. He'd been into it until he'd realized she was holding her breath and might pass out on him.

"I would love to do something about her wardrobe," Mandy said. "I think she has a good figure under those baggy clothes, but I'm not going to say a word and risk embarrassing her."

"Yeah, I wouldn't," Aunt Jo said. "She might be perfectly happy with the way things are. We shouldn't assume that everyone wants what we do."

Cody would have liked to agree with that statement, but he couldn't. Faith wasn't perfectly happy with the status quo. She knew there was something more and she wanted at least a taste of what she'd missed out on.

She wasn't looking to change herself or her life. She just wanted to experience one aspect of womanhood that intrigued her. He understood where she was coming from, but he wished like hell that she'd asked someone else to give her that experience.

Later, as everyone stood out in the yard saying their goodbyes, Zane took him aside. "What's up, bro?"

He pretended ignorance. "What do you mean?"

"She put a new starter in her truck last month. I remember that distinctly because it was cold as hell and she did it over by the barn so she could plug in a little space heater while she worked."

"Hm."

"Also, your voice sounded funny when you said it was the starter, like it does when you're stretching the truth."

Cody blew out a breath. "I can't talk about it."

"All right. I respect that. I will admit that if she loans you Bert, that would be a great solution to your horse problem."

"I know."

"Gonna take her up on it?"

"Not sure."

"Because there's a catch?"

Cody gazed at him without speaking.

Zane nodded. "There's a catch. Like they say, there's no such thing as a free horse."

"Ain't that the truth."

"Just wanted you to know if you get in a snarl, I'm right here."

Some of the weight lifted off his shoulders. "Good to know." Despite not being able to talk it out with Zane, he liked having his big brother nearby in case there was fallout.

After everyone left, he helped his mom stack the dessert plates in the dishwasher and wipe down the counters. "Thanks for inviting them over." He squeezed out the dishrag. "It was great catching up."

"I could tell. You were really into the conversation at dinner." She put soap in the dishwasher and switched it on.

"Zane and Mandy look so happy. Aunt Jo, too. To think she almost moved to New York City with Mandy."

"I know." His mom leaned against the counter. "All's well that ends well." She gestured toward her cast. "Even this has some advantages. If I hadn't broken my leg, we wouldn't have hired Faith."

"I've been thinking about that. What happens when you're back to work leading trail rides and working down at the barn?"

"Are you afraid that we'll let her go?"

"You won't need her like you do now."

His mom smiled. "Don't worry. We'll find a way to keep her on. For one thing, she's an excellent riding teacher. We could offer more lessons and that alone might be enough to pay her salary."

"Good." After seeing that tidy place Faith was so proud of, he didn't want to think of her being suddenly out of work by next fall and potentially having money problems. She could probably find something else, but she loved it here. She fit in.

"You like her, don't you?"

"Sure. Who wouldn't?"

"She must like you, too, if she'd trust you with her horse."

"Which is kind of amazing since she doesn't really know me."

"Yes, she does. You know how moms are. I talk about my boys all the time."

"Yeah, but you're prejudiced." Then he remembered something Faith had said. "Did you tell her I was a little bit spoiled?"

She looked amused. "I might have."

"Am I?"

"Not much." She came over and gave him a hug. "And if you are, it's all my fault. You were my last baby, and I treasured you."

"Because of your folks." She'd confessed one time when they were on the porch having a beer that she'd gotten pregnant soon after her parents died in a car accident. She'd wanted something joyful to think about.

"I won't deny that having you helped me through that, but I treasured you for your own self, too. You were an adorable baby. You had the chubbiest cheeks."

He rolled his eyes. "Mom."

"It's true! Maybe next time we have people over I'll get out the photo albums and prove it to you. There's one of you on a furry rug—"

"Exactly which cheeks are we talking about?"

"Both sets, actually. I really should drag out some old pictures."

"Please don't."

"We'll see." She gave him a mischievous smile that guaranteed those albums would be coming out. "Anyway, I think the next time we all get together I should invite Faith and her dad. What did you say his name was?"

"Jim, but—"

"Jim, right. I should have thought of this sooner. He's new in town and probably doesn't know many people. I'll try to organize another dinner before you leave."

"Um, okay."

"You don't sound very enthusiastic. Is there something about Jim you're not telling me?"

"No, no! He seems really nice." What a trap. He didn't know if he'd end up going along with Faith's request or not, but either way he wouldn't want to socialize with her father, for God's sake. But he had only himself to blame. He'd been the genius who'd mentioned Jim when they were all on the porch. "Inviting him over is a great idea."

"Then I'll do it." She smothered a yawn. "I'm ready to turn in. How about you?"

"You know what? I've missed sitting on the porch. I'm gonna grab a beer and go back out there for a while."

"Sounds nice. If I weren't exhausted I'd join you." Her gaze was warm. "It's good having you home, son."

"It's good to be here. Sleep tight." He watched her hobble out of the kitchen. Mostly she wore sweats because they accommodated her cast, but tonight she'd put on the jeans Mandy had created for her. They had rhinestone-studded zippers up both sides and more rhinestones on the back pockets. "You were stylin' tonight, Mom!" he called after her.

"Don't you know it, sonny boy!"

Laughing, Cody snagged a brewsky from the refrigerator and walked back out to the front porch. At twenty, he'd felt the need to leave the ranch and find a job miles away where no one knew the McGavin brothers. Not that he was ashamed of his family. He loved them all dearly.

But he'd objected to constantly being lumped in with the other four boys. Maybe it was human nature to compare five brothers who looked so much alike. He'd become sick of it.

He wasn't sick of it anymore. He liked that Zane was paying attention and had his back. Ryker would be home in August and he couldn't wait to see the guy. Bryce and Trevor were down in Texas wrangling cattle for some bigwig, but they'd be back eventually and Cody would like to be on hand when they returned.

He had an excellent job at the Triangle V, though, with good benefits and an understanding boss. Not every employer would have given him the summer off to go gallivanting around the countryside taking videos. He'd promised to do a few video presentations when he went back in September. His boss thought the adventures of a traveling cowboy might be a nice extra to offer guests.

But he wasn't out here to think about his family or his job. If he didn't make a decision about Faith before he hit the sack, he'd toss and turn all night. Leaning back in his chair, he sipped his beer.

He wished now he hadn't kissed her. But she'd looked up at him with those big green eyes and he hadn't been able to think of a graceful way out of doing it. Oh, hell, he might as well admit that he'd wanted to.

The open door had given him just enough light to make out her delicate features and the freckles splashed across her cute little nose. Her mouth, pale pink and perfectly shaped, had drawn him closer. At the time, he'd told himself it was only curiosity prodding him to kiss her, but tonight he had to be brutally honest. He'd looked at her and his body had reacted.

And there it was, the naked truth. He'd had time to think about having sex with Faith and it no longer sounded like the worst idea in the world. Mandy had said tonight she thought Faith had a good figure under those baggy clothes. Damn it all, now he wanted to find out.

Then he had to laugh at himself. He'd planned this trip hoping to explore uncharted territory. Faith was uncharted territory. That concept drew him, too, along with the obvious tug of his libido.

He finished his beer and put the bottle next to his feet. Crickets chirped in the bushes behind the house and somewhere nearby an owl hooted. Despite its name, Wild Creek Ranch provided an atmosphere of calm, of peace. If he agreed to become sexually involved with Faith, a woman with no experience and an employee besides, he could jeopardize that.

Faith might think no one would ever find out, but eventually they would. His mom and her dad might not be so pleased with his actions. Although he wouldn't be around much because of his job, he'd come home periodically and Faith would be here. Or not. If the secret came out, she might be too embarrassed to stay.

She would be disappointed when he told her no and he hated that. He'd do his best to explain the reasons so she wouldn't get her feelings hurt. He'd emphasize that his decision wasn't because he didn't want her. Now that she'd put the thought in his mind, he'd probably spend the rest of his visit in a state of semi-arousal.

He was already battling that problem. Her mouth had been so soft, so willing. He'd fought the urge to thrust his tongue inside. If he hadn't figured out she was holding her breath, he might have done it. He still wanted to, and now she understood that she was supposed to breathe...

Okay, enough. He would carefully explain why he wasn't going to do as she'd asked. He'd made his decision.

* * *

Cody timed his arrival at Faith's house for exactly seven, although he'd bet she'd been ready long before that. He had.

The minute he drove up, she hurried out the front door dressed in her usual ensemble—old boots, baggy jeans and a loose plaid shirt. Her hat was pulled down over her eyes. That was a good thing. Those eyes were more powerful than he'd originally given them credit for.

He tried to make it around to the passenger door before she did, but he failed.

"Thanks anyway." She gave him that gap-toothed smile as she closed the door and buckled her seat belt. She was nervous, though. Her cheeks were much pinker than normal, which made her freckles fade a little.

He liked those freckles. Did she have them on any other part of her body? Then he swore under his breath as he rounded the truck and got behind the wheel. That kind of thinking would get him in big trouble and he would cut it out *now.*

Closing his door, he reached for the seat belt. Something was different about her but it took him a few seconds to figure out what it was. She smelled wonderful. His hand on the ignition, he glanced over at her. "What's that perfume?"

"Do you like it?"

"I do. What's it called?"

"It's not perfume."

"That's the name of it?"

"No, that's my answer. It's not perfume. It's vanilla."

"Oh." He breathed it in. Then he leaned closer to get another whiff. Whoops. Shouldn't be doing that. He immediately backed off and cleared his throat. "You mean like vanilla scented body lotion?"

"No, I mean vanilla, like you use when you're baking cookies." She nudged back her hat and looked at him. "I dabbed it on in a few places."

He gazed into those big green eyes and was done for. He'd never be able to find the words to tell her that he couldn't be her lover. He'd dare any decent man with a soft heart to say such a hurtful thing to her. She had no clue how to seduce him, but she'd hoped that a few dabs of vanilla might do the trick. It did.

4

Judging from Cody's expression, he liked the vanilla. Faith congratulated herself on having the foresight to ask her father that important question. "So have you decided whether you're willing to deflower me?"

"That word grates on my nerves like sandpaper." He turned the key and started his truck.

"It's in a lot of my books. What sounds better? Unvirgin me?" She noticed his jaw muscles tightening and decided maybe she should shut up before she ruined the effect of the vanilla.

"In an ideal world, when a woman chooses to be with a man for the first time, she's gifting him with her virginity." He drove away from her house.

"You think of my virginity as a gift to you?"

"Yes."

"Does that mean you're willing to do it?"

"Yes."

"Woo-hoo! Awesome possum!" She lifted both arms and did a little lap dance on the passenger seat because she couldn't help herself. The vanilla had been the key to unlocking his heart, or more accurately, removing his pants. Eventually. "Can we do it tonight?"

"Uh...tonight?"

"You betcha! The clock is ticking." And the sooner they got through the first experience, the less time she'd have to endure the jitters. Celebrating her victory was the easy part. Doing the actual deed would take courage, but she was determined. She'd never have a better setup or a more beautiful man.

"Do you have a plan? Because the ranch house is out since my mom's there and you're living with your dad."

"Of course I have a plan. Like I said, I've been thinking about this for two months."

"You did say that."

She settled back in the seat, although her adrenaline level was off the charts and she had the pulse rate to prove it. "Are you taking Bert on your trip?"

"Probably, although it feels weird to be taking a horse in exchange for...for..."

"A deflowering. See, there's no good word for it in our modern language. In the books the hero sometimes refers to the woman's feminine parts as being like the petals of a flower, so I think deflowering works. I like it."

"I don't. It sounds destructive, almost violent."

"Not to me, but we're getting off track. You wanted to know my plan."

He nodded. "I do, especially if you have visions of starting tonight."

"I want to. You may not believe this, but I'm a wee bit nervous."

"I'd be worried if you weren't."

She glanced at him. "Are you nervous?"

"Of course I'm nervous! So much could go wrong."

"But it won't, because I've figured out all the details. If you're going to take Bert on your trip, then you need to become acquainted with him. You said that yourself."

"Absolutely." He slowed down as they drove through town. "I'm sure he's a great horse since you've trained him, but he might take a dislike to me for some reason."

"He won't. Bert likes everybody. But getting to know Bert is how you and I will arrange our rendezvous every evening. After I'm finished with my work at the ranch, you'll follow me home so we can take a ride into the country. Our property borders on state rangeland. Nobody but us and the cows."

"You want to do it outside?" He seemed startled by that idea.

"It sounds wonderful in the books. You've never done it outside?"

He shrugged. "A couple of times when I was a teenager. I'm warning you that the ground's not as comfortable and it's not like we can haul an innerspring mattress along on our evening rides."

"Cody McGavin, you really are spoiled!"

"I'm not either. I just—"

"Aren't you the cowboy who's leaving to explore the wilderness in a couple of weeks? You'll be sleeping on the ground, then, I'll bet."

"Sleeping on the ground is a whole different thing from having sex on the ground. That's all I'm sayin'."

"Is that a deal breaker? Because my plan was to have sex on the ground."

"It's not a deal breaker. I just think that for your first time you should be comfortable. It's special, and I'd hate to think the moment would be ruined because a sharp rock was digging into your backside."

That comment demonstrated why Cody was the perfect choice. He might not have been turned on by the prospect of a virgin like she'd hoped he would be, but now that he'd accepted her invitation, he was intent on making her deflowering memorable. "I've been to the site many times and I thought of that. I've cleared a spot and made sure the rocks are all gone."

"What about cow patties?"

"The grass is sparse in that area, so they don't generally graze there. I've never seen cow patties."

He took a deep breath. "You really have been planning this for two months." He glanced over at her. "What if I'd said no?"

"I would have been very sad."

"Would you have gone looking for another candidate? I mean, you did take out all the rocks in that one area. What a shame to let that effort go to waste."

Should she tell him the truth? Might as well. "I didn't know if I would take this step. I had the heroes in my books, and a fantasy life isn't all bad. Then I saw you."

He sucked in a breath. "Faith, I'm not some virtuoso in bed. Or on the ground, if that's where we end up. I can't promise that I'll give you the experience of a lifetime or send you on a rocket ship to the stars. I'm just a regular guy."

She smiled because he was adorable. "I've spent my life around regular guys, and not a one of them made me want to take what is, I'll admit, a huge step. But you have a smile that lights up a room, Cody. There's a reason you're so popular with the single women at the guest ranch. You make them believe in the fantasy."

"Good Lord, I'm not—"

"Yes, you are, at least for me. That leaves only one question. Can we do this tonight?"

He swallowed. "Yes, ma'am."

* * *

Cody was in the soup, now, and all day he alternated between excitement and dread. His mom would have a fit if she knew what he'd agreed to, so he avoided her as much as possible. Fortunately, he needed to run several errands in town, so after he'd made sure the basic chores had been done at the barn, he left Wild Creek Ranch with a sense of relief.

In April, he'd ordered a camper shell for his truck. He'd wanted one in midnight blue with silver pin striping to match the truck's paint job, and the

Ford dealer had called to say it had come in. They installed it for him, although once the trip was over he'd want to take it off and store it...somewhere. He wasn't sure where that would be, but he'd work that out when the time came.

The camper shell made the trip real. Until it had been fitted to his truck bed, he hadn't formed a clear picture of what he hoped to achieve. The shell provided a temporary home and he spent the rest of the day picking up what might be called home furnishings.

When he was finished, the truck bed had been transformed into a cozy hideaway with a cushy mattress, sheets and blankets, and several pillows. He also bought a lantern and a single-person tent. He expected to be in that tent during most of his travels, but when he returned to his truck, he wanted a touch of luxury.

Last of all, he stopped by the drugstore. He'd focused on his trip all morning and had managed to keep thoughts of tonight at bay. But he couldn't ignore the item he'd need for the task he'd perform in a few hours. No, he shouldn't call it a task. He needed to think of it as a privilege. He hoped to give her some pleasure. She deserved that.

He wasn't enthralled with her plan of making love on the ground, though. Had they both been driven by lust, then yeah, any horizontal surface would do. Or vertical surface.

But sex with Faith wouldn't be like that. He'd need to take his time and gradually ease her into the experience. That kind of approach worked better on an innerspring. In any case, he'd need condoms. He parked in front of Pills and Pop, an old-fashioned drugstore that still had a soda fountain and a reconditioned jukebox.

Eagles Nest was up to date where it counted, with cell reception and Wi-Fi in most areas. Their top-notch little hospital had a knowledgeable staff and the small police department was vigilant. The fire department was mostly volunteer, but Cody would put them up against any outfit in the country. His brother Trevor planned to take the training when he came back from Texas.

Pills and Pop, though, was pure fifties nostalgia. It was a first date kind of place, where you could buy a girl a milkshake and find out if you had the same taste in music. Cody and his brothers had learned to dance on the linoleum in front of the jukebox. His mom and her friends had, too, back when they were teenagers.

Cody had bought his first package of condoms here and he'd gradually learned not to be embarrassed about shopping for that item. He wasn't embarrassed now, either. Instead he was worried that the event would lack romance.

So after choosing a package from the rack by the pharmacy department, he cruised the aisles looking for inspiration. Eventually he paused beside a display of scented candles in small glass holders.

"Your mom would like those."

He turned at the husky sound of a smoker's voice. Ellie Mae Stockton had worked at Pills and Pop ever since he could remember. He'd once asked his mom how old she thought Ellie Mae was. They'd calculated that she had to be past eighty, and that had been a couple of years ago.

But Ellie Mae took good care of herself. Her short hair was colored a soft brown and her makeup had been carefully applied. She'd buried two husbands and swore she'd never remarry unless a billionaire came along.

"You're looking great, Ellie Mae."

"So are you, Cody." Then she spied the condoms in his hand and laughed. "I see now why you're thinking about those candles. What scent does the lady prefer?"

"Vanilla."

"You're in luck. Those cream-colored ones are vanilla. How many do you want?"

"I'll take all four."

"Is that enough? I might have some in the back if you want to make a splash."

"I do."

"Then I'll see if we have more." She hurried away.

He wasn't being very stealthy. If someone he knew caught him standing there with condoms and candles, they'd take note of it. Word might get around and Faith didn't want that. He put the candles back on the shelf and wandered away from the display.

No sooner had he made that move than Aunt Jo came around the end of the aisle, probably on a lunch break from her job at the bank. "Hey, Aunt Jo!"

"I knew you were in here." She gave him a hug. "That truck of yours really stands out. The camper shell is gorgeous and your truck looks brand new!"

"They washed the truck after they put the camper on. And thanks for that cake last night. It was awesome."

"Baked it just for you."

"I know and I appreciate it." He'd always thought she looked like a classy movie star with her super-short gray hair and big hoop earrings.

She glanced down at the condom package in his hand. "Supplies for the trip?"

"Uh, no. Just...stocking up."

Her eyes twinkled. "Okey-doke. Didn't mean to pry."

"Cody, I found four more boxes of vanilla!" Ellie Mae came from the opposite direction. "You can make a real splash with twenty candles!"

His face heated as he took the boxes from her. "I can, at that." He glanced at Aunt Jo, who was regarding him with amusement. "I'm going to ask both of you ladies to do me a huge favor and not tell anyone about me buying these candles and...condoms."

"Ooo, a secret rendezvous!" Ellie Mae clasped her hands together. "My lips are sealed."

Aunt Jo nodded. "Mine, too."

"You can't tell anyone, Aunt Jo, but especially not Mom or Mandy."

"I've kept your secrets before, Cody McGavin. I can keep this one."

"Thank you."

"You don't have to worry about me, either," Ellie Mae said. "The whole town comes in here for one thing or another and everybody has something to hide. I don't talk about any of it. That's their business."

"I'm grateful to both of you. Listen, I'd better pay for all this and get on home. Mom texted me earlier and she's eager to see how the camper shell turned out." He managed to leave the store without further incident, but he'd learned a lesson about secret affairs. They could get complicated fast.

He stashed the candles and the condoms behind the pillows at the far end of the mattress. Just his luck if he left them on the passenger seat someone would see them and ask questions. He could deflect any questions about the condoms, but twenty vanilla scented candles would arouse curiosity.

As he drove past the arena on his way up to the house, Faith and Mandy were out there with Licorice, the horse that had thrown his mom. Somebody had spoiled that mare by making her into a pet and then they'd sold her to a clueless family with a twelve-year-old daughter. His mom had been trying to teach Licorice manners when the mare had caught her unawares and pitched her in the dirt.

Zane had wanted the horse transferred to a different stable, probably still did, but their mom wouldn't hear of it. Mandy had taken up the cause and now Faith had become part of Team Licorice. Cody decided to park his truck and walk down there before bringing his mom out to admire the camper shell.

They'd put the mare on a lunge line. Mandy cantered Licorice in a circle while Faith held the line and pivoted slowly as she watched the horse. Mandy waved to him but Faith kept her attention on Licorice. Cody tugged his hat a little lower so he could observe Faith without being obvious about it.

Tendrils of hair had escaped her braid to curl against the back of her neck and her shirt collar gapped enough that he could admire the gentle curve of her throat. He'd never paid attention to the way she moved, but she possessed the grace and confidence of a natural athlete.

She dressed like a rough and tumble boy, but tonight he might discover a delicately made woman under those bulky clothes. If he had to guess, he'd say her underwear would be plain white cotton with no frills. He'd find out. And he'd learn what she looked like with nothing on at all.

Okay, maybe he was excited about this encounter, because he was turning himself on with the slide show going in his head. He would be the first man allowed to touch her in a sexual way, to watch her nipples tighten and her eyes grow dark with passion.

"Cody." Mandy's voice was soft but it carried across the arena.

His head came up. "What?"

"You need to leave."

"Why?"

"I can feel her tensing up."

At first he thought she was talking about Faith, but then he realized she meant Licorice. "She still doesn't like men?"

"We thought she was getting better, but I think she just noticed you and…whoops, here we go." She grabbed a hunk of mane as Licorice bucked.

Cody took his cue and backed away from the arena. Just as well. Any more time spent leaning against the fence imagining Faith naked was liable to give him a woody and embarrass everyone.

He walked up to the house and let his mom know he was ready to show off the new camper shell.

She finished up what she was doing and came out. Hobbling around the truck, she admired it from all angles. "Gorgeous, Cody. The camper shell is perfect, as if it came with the truck. They must have washed it for you."

"Yep."

"You should video it against a wilderness background on your first day before it gets dirty."

"Great idea. Then I'll take another one at the end of the trip when it's covered in grime."

"Yeah, and if for some reason it doesn't look dirty enough, just drive through some mud on purpose."

He laughed. "Good thinking."

Her eyes sparkled as she gazed at him. "I can't wait to watch that video. You're finally making your dream come true."

"Sure am. I almost can't believe it."

"Well, believe it. All you need is a trailer. I'm sure the right one will turn up soon."

"Hope so."

She peered in the side window of the camper shell. "What's in the back? Did you get bedding?"

"I did." He opened the back window and the tailgate so she could examine his setup.

"Wow, this looks so inviting." She smoothed her hand over the blanket. "You won't be roughing it when you sleep in here."

"I figured I might need a break from lying on the ground."

"Speaking of that, will you have any way of keeping in touch when you're out there in the wilds?"

"I will if there's cell reception. I bought a solar charger for my phone so I can take selfies and send them to you."

"Do that." She gazed at him for a long moment and then she cleared her throat. "Take lots of selfies, okay?"

"Don't worry. I'll be in contact whenever I can." He gave her shoulder a squeeze. Then he reached for the tailgate to close it up.

"Wait a sec." His mom stopped him. "Mandy and Faith are coming out of the barn. Leave it open so they can see it." She made a megaphone of her hands. "Hey, come look at Cody's setup!"

"On our way!" Mandy called back. She beamed at him as they drew closer. "Gorgeous camper shell."

"Thanks."

"Wait'll you see how he's fixed up the back." His mom gestured toward the opening.

Mandy peered inside. "That is so cool. You did a great job." She stepped back. "Take a gander, Faith."

Cody's heart rate picked up. Standing here with Faith while she inspected the bed he'd created was giving him ideas that heated his skin. If that heat reached his face, he'd be in trouble.

"It does look nice." Her voice was soft and a little shaky. She kept her head slightly down, too, so her hat obscured her expression.

He took his cue from her and tugged his hat lower. Would he have a chance to share this bed with her before he left? He would love to, but he couldn't think about it now.

A breeze picked up, cooling his overheated skin as the sun disappeared behind a cloud. A rumble of thunder followed.

His mom glanced toward the mountains. "Looks like that storm they predicted is coming in early."

"What storm?" Cody had been too preoccupied to check the weather.

"A big one," Mandy said. "It wasn't supposed to start raining until tonight, but I think Aunt Kendra's right. You'd better button up your rolling motel room. Me, I'm heading back home before it hits."

"Good idea," his mom said. "Faith, if you want to beat the storm home, Cody and I can handle feeding tonight."

Faith gazed at the sky. "If it's coming in early, maybe it'll be gone by feeding time."

"Hang on." Mandy pulled out her phone. "Let me check. Nope, the weather app says it'll keep up most of the night."

"And Wagon Wheel Road has that place that floods in June when the snow's melting in the mountains." Cody had seen it running and he didn't want her driving through it.

"How do you know it floods in June?" Faith studied him.

"He used to have a girlfriend who lived out there," his mom said. "I'd worry myself sick whenever they were on a date and it started to pour."

"Oh." Faith gave him a quick glance and then took a deep breath. "Then I'd better vamoose. See you all later."

"See you tomorrow," he called after her. Their plans were wrecked. Damn.

5

Faith ate a quick dinner with her dad, pretended exhaustion and escaped upstairs to her room. Rain came down in sheets outside her window, and she yanked the curtains closed to blot out the sight. Why hadn't she checked the weather report?

Because she'd been rattled. After focusing all her efforts on getting Cody to say yes, he had. Once the glow of triumph had passed, she'd had hours to get nervous. He'd left after chores were done and she'd appreciated that.

But then he'd come back and she was convinced her nerves had spooked Licorice, not Cody's presence. He'd been watching her. Her brain had gone a little crazy trying to imagine what he'd been thinking.

But if the stupid storm hadn't blown in, they would have already done the deed in the little clearing she'd found. The area where she'd dug up rocks and raked until it was smooth was probably fit for mud wrestling. She had almost twenty-four hours to wait for the main event, assuming he was willing to reschedule.

Almost twenty-four hours in which to get even more jittery at the prospect of being naked with a gorgeous cowboy. She was too restless to sleep, so she took a hot bath and shaved her legs, the second time in two days. She ducked her head under the faucet, washed her hair and then dried it, which took forever when the humidity was so high. She braided it again.

Finally, she put on her sleep shorts and tank top, picked out a book from the box under her bed and settled down to read as rain sluiced down outside. The story turned out to be one of the hotter ones about a duke and a widow and she smiled at the thought of Mrs. Preston, a stately matriarch, reading it.

The sexy parts made her squirm in her bed. She wished that Cody could magically appear in her room, but that wouldn't happen, so she kept reading. The steady rain soothed her and she eventually drifted off to sleep.

Naturally she dreamed about Cody, who had transformed into a duke living in England, with a mansion and servants. It was a good dream, and the hail bouncing off her window was annoying. If it didn't stop, she was going to wake up. Oh, no, she was awake, blinking in the light from the bedside lamp she'd left on, and the dream was drifting away…

The hail kept hitting her window, but it didn't sound like any hail she'd heard before. One hailstone would strike the glass and a second later, another one made contact, almost as if someone was throwing it. She listened more carefully and her eyes widened.

Jumping out of bed, she pulled back the curtains and looked down at the rectangle of light cast by her window. Cody McGavin.

His hat was shoved back as he gazed up and smiled at her. He wore a black suede jacket that made his broad shoulders look even wider, especially from this angle. She pinched herself to make sure she wasn't still dreaming.

She shoved the window open. Cool, moist air wafted against her skin, but the rain had stopped. She kept her voice down. "What are you doing?"

"Trying to get your attention. Your light was on. Were you awake?"

"No. I fell asleep reading."

"Oh, sorry. I couldn't sleep and thought maybe you couldn't either. My bad."

"Come around to the front door. I'll be out."

"Listen, you can go back to sleep. I'll leave."

"Don't you dare!" Heart pounding, she pulled on a jacket and picked up her boots. He'd come for her. How dashing was that?

She switched off the light in her room, slipped out into the hall and crept down the stairs. Her dad was a heavy sleeper but she didn't want to take any chance that she'd wake him. Moving quickly through the darkened living room, she leaned against the wall to tug on her boots. Then she opened the front door and walked out on the porch.

Light from a lamp mounted next to the door gleamed on the puddles in the yard and the raindrops clinging to the leaves and the pine needles nearby. The air smelled fresh, with a touch of damp earth mixed in. Cody waited just below the steps. Seeing him there made her breath catch.

"I didn't mean to wake you up." His voice was soft as moonlight.

"I don't care." She paused at the top of the steps. "But you still haven't told me why you're here." She had some idea, but she wanted to be sure.

"I was disappointed that our plan was spoiled."

"Me, too."

"When the rain stopped, I wondered if we could work things out, anyway."

Adrenaline shot through her system, making her quiver. "How? We can't take the horses out now, and anyway, the ground is a soggy mess."

"I know." He held out his hand. "I came up with an alternative."

She maneuvered down the steps cautiously. Her work boots made more noise because they were loose on her feet. She usually wore socks with them. "I don't want my dad to wake up."

"Do you think he will?"

"Probably not." She put her hand in his. Oh, that felt good. "The week we moved in, a pair of owls were doing their mating ritual in the pine tree that's right beside his bedroom. They were loud. They woke me up and I stayed awake until they quit. The next day my dad said he hadn't heard a thing."

He squeezed her hand. "Then we should be okay."

"Where's your truck?"

He laced his fingers through hers. "A little way down the road. When I walked here, the moon gave me plenty of light to see, but it's chilly. Are you cold?"

"I'm too excited to be cold."

"Okay." As they started walking, he drew in a breath. "Listen, I need to tell you that…the first time…there can be pain."

"I've heard that but I don't think it will be a problem for me."

"Why not?"

"I've spent most of my life on a horse. I've read that constant riding can eliminate that situation. But I just thought of something. If I don't have pain, will you think I'm lying about being a virgin?"

"No, I'd never think that. You're too honest."

"I'm not, either. I told you my starter was going out when it wasn't."

He pulled her around to face him. "Let's settle this. Did you make up the story about being a virgin to get me into bed?"

"No."

"Good enough for me." He started down the road again, his hand gripping hers.

"Let me ask you something."

"Shoot."

"Yesterday you were freaked out by my request but I sense a change in your attitude."

He chuckled. "Do you, now?"

"You seem much more enthusiastic tonight. How come?"

"Maybe it took me a while to realize what a gift you're offering. The idea has been growing on me ever since yesterday. Being the first one is a privilege, but I'd be less than honest if I didn't admit it's a turn-on, too."

"So the books were right about that."

"I can't say. Haven't read them."

"Well, I have, and in those books, virginity is a big deal. When a man claims a virgin, it's like they're bonded for life."

"Hang on." He planted his feet in the loamy soil. "Is that what you're after? A lifetime bond?"

"No, silly. I already told you this is a temporary deal. We each have our lives set up the way we want them so why mess with that?"

He continued to study her. "But what if you find out you really like it?"

"I hope to Hannah I'll like it. This is my only shot so I want it to be good."

"That's my point. What if it's so freaking wonderful that you want to keep doing it for longer than two weeks?"

"I doubt that."

For some reason, he found that funny. "How can you be so sure?"

"Easy. Judging from all the books I've read, it's exciting the first few times, but then the story has to end because after that it gets boring. It's just wash, rinse, repeat."

He let go of her hand and held his sides because he was laughing so hard. "Wash, rinse, repeat." He gasped for air and wiped his eyes. "I hate that I'll never be able to tell anyone you said that. It's hysterical."

"Cody, you promised me that you—"

"I won't. I swear I won't, but Zane would crack up." He cleared the laughter from his throat but he still looked highly amused. "If you're so sure it gets boring, why bother at all?"

"Because I want to experience the first part, when everything's shiny and new. At least it'll be new for me. It could end up being old hat for you."

"Somehow I don't think so."

"Only because you've never done it with me, so that'll be different."

"Guaranteed."

"Anyway, from my point of view, once the mystery's gone, I'll be over it."

"Then we'd better proceed with the program so you can check it off your list." He recaptured her hand. "By the way, I have a surprise for you."

"What's that?"

"When we get around the next bend in the road, you'll see."

A minute later she gasped with delight. "Oh, *Cody*. That's so beautiful!" He'd swung the truck around and opened the back. Candles flickered on the ground on either side, turning the clearing into a fairyland. Soft lantern light illuminated the cozy bed she'd seen earlier today.

As she took in the romantic setting, she became aware of a sweet aroma blending with the fresh scent of rain and wet pine needles. Dazzled, she turned to him. "The candles are scented."

"Vanilla."

Swallowing, she gazed at him and hoped she wouldn't tear up. "No one…no one has ever done something like this for me."

"Then it's about time."

* * *

Cody would remember this night for the rest of his life. Faith was looking at him as if he'd hung the moon, and all he'd done was tuck a small lantern in the corner of the camper shell and light a few candles. Thank God Ellie Mae had mentioned having more in the back room, though. Four wouldn't have had the same impact.

But twenty made a splash, like Ellie Mae had said, especially for someone who'd read stories about romantic gestures but had never personally experienced any. He enjoyed the heck out of her delight and gratitude. Not every guy had a chance to be this kind of hero.

Also, Mandy was probably right about Faith. Those baggy clothes disguised a great figure. She'd come out on the porch wearing sleep shorts and boots, which left a good bit of her legs exposed. If the rest of her was as shapely as her legs, he was in for a treat.

She held his gaze, her expression eager and open. "What happens next?"

Once again, she made him smile. "For a virgin, you sure are fearless."

"I'm not totally fearless. My insides are shaking."

"So are mine."

"You're scared?"

"Not scared. Aroused."

"By me?"

"Yes, ma'am."

She glanced down at her outfit. "I can't imagine why. There's nothing sexy to see here."

"Wanna bet?" Spanning her waist with both hands, he swung her up to the tailgate so quickly that she squeaked. "Here's what's sexy. Finally getting to see your legs, or most of them."

"My legs turn you on?"

Stepping back, he surveyed her sitting there. Nice. "You have very pretty knees."

"Nobody's ever told me that."

"Likely because you never show them off."

"Ranch hands don't go around showing off their knees. I'm positive you don't."

"Mine aren't as pretty as yours." Moving closer, he cupped a knee in each hand and gazed into her eyes. "Or as soft." He massaged gently.

"That feels nice."

"Good." He stroked the tops of her thighs. "How's that?"

"I like it." Her voice trembled slightly.

He moved her thighs apart and eased between them. "Can I undo your braid?"

"My hair will go everywhere."

"That's the idea. I've never seen it loose."

"Okay." She flipped her braid over her shoulder and pulled off the elastic on the end. "I can—"

"Let me. I've never touched your hair, either." Slowly he unwound the red-gold strands and allowed them to slide through his fingers. "Like silk." When he was finished, he combed it out with his fingers, massaging her scalp and watching as her eyes lost focus and her breathing grew shallow. He wondered if she'd ever experienced the sensuality of having someone fool with her hair.

Careful not to break the spell, he leaned forward and kept his voice low. "Want to try kissing?"

She nodded.

He laid his hat on the tailgate. He'd fantasized about her mouth ever since that first taste and anticipation thrummed in his veins as he closed in. Then he paused. The spell must have been broken after all, because now she was giving him a laser-like stare. He pulled back. "Close your eyes."

They snapped shut. "Forgot."

God, she was adorable. "You can leave them open if you want, but personally I like shutting off the visual so I can concentrate on the kiss."

"I want to do that, too."

"Don't forget to breathe this time. If I end up calling the paramedics our secret will be out."

"Got it."

If engineering a kiss took this long, they would be here all night getting to the main event. That was fine with him. She was becoming more delicious by the second. But he'd have to exercise a truckload of control if he expected to be the man she needed.

He slowly touched down on the plump contours of lips perfect for kissing. But she didn't know it yet. When he'd been playing spin-the-bottle at his first boy-girl party, she'd been learning how to throw a rope and string barbed wire. She was a better hand than he was, but he knew more about kissing and this was a teaching moment.

He cradled her jaw and lifted his head slightly. "Are you breathing?"

"Yes." Her voice was a mere whisper. "More kissing, please."

"Open your mouth a little."

She murmured something.

"I didn't hear that."

Her eyes stayed closed but she smiled. "You want to put your tongue in there, don't you?"

"Do you care?"

"Oh, no, I want you to. That's part of it."

"You can put yours in my mouth, too."

"At the same time?"

"Absolutely."

Her eyelids fluttered open. "How does that work?"

"I have no idea, but it does. I'll start and you can join in when you feel ready." He returned to her mouth and his pulse rate kicked up several notches as he slowly slipped his tongue inside her warmth. She was so lush. He explored gently and then took the kiss deeper.

She flattened both hands against his chest as if she was about to push him away, but instead she grabbed hold of his shoulders. She'd remembered to breathe. In fact, she was almost panting.

The first slide of her tongue against his sent a message straight to his groin. He sucked on her tongue. She quickly returned the favor. The woman had instinctive talent, and his fevered brain began painting scenarios in which he'd teach her where else she could employ that talent. His jeans began to pinch and he didn't come to his senses until he'd reached for the tab on his zipper.

Easing away from that hot kiss, he gasped for breath.

She was gulping in air, too. "That...was fun. Let's...let's do it some more."

"We can't."

"Why not?"

"Because kissing you like that makes me want to rush things." His chest heaved. "I don't want to rush things." But he stripped off his jacket and tossed it into the camper because he sure didn't need the extra layer anymore.

"We can rush things. That's okay with me." Mirroring him, she shimmied out of her jacket and threw it on top of his. "What's next?"

He gave her a quick glance. Then he drew in a sharp breath and stared. She wore a stretchy white tank top that concealed nothing. The sleep shorts looked skimpy, too, now that the jacket wasn't obscuring his view. Holy hell. The woman was built like a goddess and once she'd ditched the jacket, all that bounty was on display, including erect nipples that poked against the material and begged to be touched.

"Cody, are you okay?"

He nodded and tried to form words, but his tongue was stuck to the roof of his mouth.

"You don't look okay. You look as if somebody just jabbed you with a cattle prod."

Turning away, he scrubbed a hand over his face and took several deep breaths. Then he faced her again. "Do you..." He paused to clear his throat. "Do you have any idea how beautiful you are?"

"No."

"Didn't think so." If she had, she would have made more of a production of taking off her jacket. He gestured toward her. "Seeing you in that outfit..." He propped his hands on his hips and gazed up at the stars for inspiration. "Let's just say it's testing my control."

She glanced down at herself. "Really?"

"Really. You're new at this and I want to take things slow." He gazed at her and swallowed. "That won't be easy."

"Are you going crazy with lust?" She sounded delighted.

"Yes, Faith, I'm going crazy with lust."

"Is that why you have that bulge in your jeans?"

"Yes. Yes, it is."

"Does it hurt when that happens?"

"Sometimes."

"Like now?"

"Yes."

She reached down, pulled off her boots and let them fall to the ground. Next she grabbed her tank top and yanked it over her head. Last of all, she lifted her hips and whipped off her sleep shorts. “Then let’s get down to business.”

6

Faith was thrilled with how this episode was going. She never would have guessed that her tank top and sleep shorts would have the same effect on a man as a beautiful ball gown or a black negligee. Their kiss involving tongues had made her more hot and bothered than any of the scenes she'd read in her books, but she also knew that nothing could happen between them unless Cody was primed for action.

Judging from how quickly he was undressing, he was indeed primed. Crawling toward the front of the truck bed, she snagged the lantern and brought it with her as she returned to the tailgate. Then she held it up so she could get a better view of Cody shucking his clothes.

He'd already taken off his shirt, his boots and his socks. She admired the solid muscles that flexed whenever he moved. Although she'd seen men without their shirts many times, very few of them had looked like Cody. He stood barefoot in a damp patch of grass, probably because he didn't want to get his feet muddy. She could understand that. He wouldn't want to get mud on his new sheets.

He paused with his hands at his belt buckle. "I don't need the light. I can see what I'm doing."

"But I can't."

"Excuse me?"

"I've seen a few pictures here and there, but never a naked man in person, let alone a fully aroused one. This could be my one and only chance. I don't want to miss it in case you don't enjoy this and decide to call it quits after one time."

"That won't be the case if it's up to me. But you might get bored." He unbuckled his belt and unfastened the button on his jeans. "You know—wash, rinse, repeat." He shoved his jeans and briefs down in one smooth movement and stepped out of them. "You'll have to be the judge of that."

Faith gulped. "Wow."

"Maybe I'm nothing special." He walked toward her, his cock jutting proudly from a thick mat of dark hair. His balls hung heavy between his thighs. "You have no basis of comparison."

"That's true." She couldn't stop looking at him. His desire was so *visible.* She ached with an intensity that startled her. "But you seem plenty large to me. Maybe I should reconsider. I don't think you'll fit."

His gaze swept over her. "I think I will. But we'll take it easy. I'm not going to hurt you."

"I didn't think so, either, until you took off your pants."

His smile held a trace of male pride. "I'm glad you're not disappointed."

"Only if this means we can't do it because you need a woman with more room."

"Give me a little time and I'll make room. The condoms are tucked behind the pillows. I'd be obliged if you'd fetch them."

"Will a condom compress you so you're smaller?" She crawled to the front of the truck bed and found the package. "That would be good."

"I'm afraid condoms don't work that way. If they did, men would never use them. Listen, I promise this will turn out better than you think. If you're as excited as I am, you'll be very wet. I'll slide right in."

"I've noticed I'm kind of juicy."

"Good." He took the package she handed him and opened it. "I can help you with that."

"How?"

"Oral sex. Wasn't that in your books?"

Her heart beat faster. "You mean when the man puts his head between her legs?"

"Uh-huh."

"Would you want to?"

"I would love to. That would be a good way to start, so I know you've had an orgasm." He opened one of the envelopes and rolled on the condom.

The condom fascinated her, too. "I've considered giving myself an orgasm."

"But you haven't?"

"No. It didn't seem important until I started reading those books, and then I really wanted my first one to be with a man."

His gaze held hers. "Then we're going to make that happen." Putting his bare foot on the bumper, he pulled himself into her space.

He took up a lot of it, too. She couldn't understand how a naked man could seem so much larger than one who was dressed, but Cody appeared huge when he joined her in the camper shell, and not just because he had such a large cock. Maybe it was all that muscle revealed instead of covered by a shirt and jeans. She wanted to touch him, but being this close to a naked man was so out of her experience that she didn't know where to begin.

She threw herself on his mercy. "Tell me what to do. I'm not sure how this is supposed to go."

Turning toward her, he gathered her close, skin against skin. "You're not supposed to know." Carefully he laid her down on the soft blanket. "I am."

Her body hummed with excitement as she waited for him to close the tailgate and the back window.

He retrieved the lantern and set it in the corner near her head. "Is that light in your eyes?"

"No." She gazed up at him. "Thank you for bringing it. I didn't want my first time to be in the dark, although I didn't know that until now."

"I was hoping you'd feel that way." Leaning down, he feathered a kiss over her mouth. "Now lie back and let me love you. If I do anything you don't like, tell me. Otherwise, relax and let it happen."

"That's easy."

He stroked a finger over her cheek. "Easy is how I want it for you. As for me, I get to explore. And find out if you have freckles in interesting places."

"I have freckles in various places, but I don't think they're interesting."

"They are to me." He kissed the tip of her nose, the edge of her chin, and each earlobe.

"Are you still crazed with lust?"

"Yes."

"Then you should relieve the pressure. We can mess around later."

"I want to mess around now."

"But—"

"Shush, Faith. This is your first time. Revel in it." And he began a lazy journey down her body.

She'd never felt anything to compare with being kissed all over by Cody McGavin. She doubted he missed a single inch, and he paid special attention to her breasts, which turned out to be very sensitive. He even insisted that she roll over so he could leave a trail of kisses down her spine, over her shoulder blades, and on her bottom. He nipped her there, too, because he said he couldn't help it.

He pressed his lips to the backs of her knees and the soles of her feet. He dipped his tongue into her belly button and licked between her toes. With every moment, she grew hotter and more restless. She'd been worried that he wouldn't fit, but the longer he delayed, the less she worried and the more she wanted him to try and make that magical connection that the books talked about.

Her pulse raced and her body writhed against the blanket. "Are you still crazed by lust?" she asked in desperation.

"Yes."

"Then do it!"

"Not yet." He kissed his way along her inner thigh.

She trembled when she figured out where he would end up. Then he placed his mouth against the very part of her that throbbed with wanting him. She couldn't imagine this would help the situation, but then he began to nuzzle and lick her there. Okay, maybe she'd been mistaken. What he was doing felt amazing.

But she wasn't sure about the sensations in her body. She began to pant. "Cody!"

"What?"

"I feel like there's a spring tightening inside me! Is that normal?"

"It's normal. You're going to come." He went back to working magic with his mouth and tongue.

"Cody!"

"What?"

"There's so much pressure! Like I'm going to explode!"

His soft chuckle warmed her damp skin. "Then explode, Faith. Let go." And he pushed deeper, cupping her bottom in both hands and opening her to his sweet assault.

When it happened, when the tremors began and the spasms rolled through her, she wondered if she was going to die. It was that strong.

But even though she cried out, he didn't seem concerned. He just held her tight and murmured soft words that tickled the sensitive skin of her inner thighs.

The sensations gradually slowed and then stopped. He slid up her sweat-soaked body and kissed her. "Congratulations."

"That was it?"

"That was it."

"I loved it."

"Knew you would."

"What's next?"

He gazed into her eyes. "We could stop now and pick up again tomorrow night."

"And leave you in your crazed lust condition?"

"I can manage."

"Manage with me. Let's see if you fit."

His cheek dented in a half smile. "I don't have a doubt in the world, but I don't want to overload your circuits."

"You won't. This is the night. It's supposed to happen now. I can feel it."

He studied her for several long seconds. "Okay. But I want you on top, so you can control everything."

"But I don't know what I'm doing."

"You might be surprised. You know more than you think." After giving her a slow, lingering kiss, he stretched out on his back. "Riding is what you do. Climb on."

She pushed herself to a sitting position and surveyed the impressive expanse of male beauty that was Cody McGavin. "I'm totally intimidated. You're an amazing specimen and I'm not experienced enough to take charge of your pleasure."

"You're taking charge of yours. Mine's not the critical part of this."

"But I want you to have fun, too."

"I will. I'm already having a blast. You reduced me to a mass of throbbing hormones just by taking off your jacket."

"That still blows me away. I sleep in that kind of outfit all summer. There's no lace, no ribbons, no peek-a-boo cutout. It's basic and uninteresting."

"Until you put it on this body." He cupped her breast and brushed his thumb over her nipple. "Then that basic outfit becomes dynamite."

"Totally unplanned." His touch created tension low in her belly, and now she knew where that could lead. She wanted that feeling again. "I had no idea you'd show up."

"That's what makes it special. You weren't trying to drive me insane. This is the real you, and you're sexy as hell."

"I doubt it, but tonight I feel that way."

"Then prove it. Take what you need from me."

"And give you what you need?"

He smiled. "You will, without even trying."

"Here goes nothing." She rose to her knees and straddled his hips.

"Here goes something. Something wonderful." He gazed up at her. "I love this view."

He arranged her hair over her breasts. "Lady Godiva."

"Mm." She didn't have the breath or the brain power to make conversation. His cock rising between her legs was a stirring sight, but she couldn't possibly take it all in.

"Just get started," he murmured.

"Can I grab hold?"

"Sure."

"I won't hurt you?"

"No."

Once she got a grip, she marveled at how hard he was. And warm. Even if she only managed halfway, that would still feel good. She braced her other hand on his chest for balance and glanced at his face. His jaw was clenched. "Are you sure I'm not hurting you?"

He choked out a laugh. "You're not."

"Then why do you look so fierce?"

"Trying not to come."

"Oh. I should get started."

"Take your time."

She didn't think he meant that. He sounded like a man under considerable strain. Holding his cock firmly, she lowered her hips. As he'd predicted, the blunt tip slid in easily, but she paused to take a breath. The fit was snug, but she immediately felt the advantage of that. The tension in her body ramped up about a thousand percent. Now that she was anchored, she put her other hand on his chest.

He gazed up at her. "How're you doing?"

"Good." She swallowed. "Even if I can't go all the way, I can make you happy, right?"

"You're making me happy, now."

She smiled. "You sound gravelly."

"You sound breathless."

"It's a big moment."

"It is." He cupped her cheek.

"And you have a big—"

"How do you know?" He gave her a wicked grin. "Maybe I'm on the lower end of the scale."

"If that's true, then God help the women of the world."

"It's not true. I'm teasing you. Trying to help you relax."

"I figured. Okay, I'm moving down some more." As she did, she closed her eyes because she wanted to concentrate on the sensations rocketing through her body. Heat and friction were a powerful combination. She liked this. No, she didn't just like it. She loved it.

His deep groan prompted her to check out how he was doing. His eyes were squeezed shut and he'd grabbed a handful of the blanket in each fist. She was torturing the poor guy, just like he'd said.

When she glanced down, she was surprised to see that she was almost there. Imagine that. The sight of them joined together filled her with an elemental urge so strong and compelling that she couldn't resist. Time to go for it. With a soft cry, she plunged the rest of the way. The sudden movement touched off her orgasm.

Gasping, she leaned forward, hands braced on his sweat-slick chest as waves of pleasure rolled through her. His big hands clutched her bottom and he held her tight against him. His hips bucked once and he yelled real loud. She'd never heard a man come before, but quite likely she just had.

No telling how long they stayed like that, each of them shaking and struggling to breathe. But at least her heartbeat slowed to a semi-normal pace. Her hair had fallen forward, curtaining her face. Tucking it behind her ears, she peeked down at him.

He was watching her, his expression intense. "Are you okay?"

"No."

Distress clouded his eyes. "Oh, Faith, I—"

"I'm way more than okay! I'm feeling fabulous! Incredible! That was the best thing that's ever happened to me!"

"Yeah?" His broad smile made the corners of his eyes crinkle. "No pain?"

"Not a bit. Cody, I can't thank you enough. I'm only sorry that it was so boring for you."

"Are you kidding?"

"I can't believe you had any fun. In my books, there's all this thrusting going on and you didn't get to do any of that."

He chuckled. "Seems as if I don't need all that thrusting. This was the best climax I've ever had."

She studied him. "Don't just say that to make me feel better."

"It's the truth. But we can try some thrusting tomorrow night, if you want."

Joy spread through her like sunshine. "You want to do this some more?"

"I'd like that a lot."

"How about now? I mean, you fit. It's tight, but you do, so—"

"I'm tempted, but you'll be happier if we wait. I'd never forgive myself if I made you sore because we overdid it the first time."

"I would forgive you." Leaning down, she brushed her sensitized nipples over his chest because it felt really good. "I think we should try it again, only with thrusting."

"Faith Underwood, are you seducing me?"

"I don't know how."

"Are you sure? Because you're doing it."

"I am?"

"Yes, you are. Using that husky tone of voice, talking dirty, rubbing your breasts against me while giving me a smokin' hot look with those big green eyes. That's seduction."

"Well, put feathers in my hair and call me a dust mop! I had no idea I was seducing you. Then are we staying?"

"No." He grinned at her. "But you're welcome to try that routine another time."

"All righty, I will." She'd always thought seduction was complicated, something she'd have to learn and practice before she'd be good at it. Apparently not.

7

Cody walked Faith home, his arm wrapped securely around her shoulders. When no lights shone from inside the house, he was relieved. He hadn't really expected her dad to be waiting on the porch with a shotgun, but it wasn't every day that a guy eliminated the virginal status of a man's only daughter. Most fathers wouldn't believe it was her idea, either.

She asked him to stop walking when they were still several yards from the front porch. "I want to kiss you goodnight, so let's stay in the shadows, just in case. Then I'll go on alone."

"Works for me. I don't have any wish to speak with your dad tonight."

"He wouldn't be mean about it." She turned into his arms. "But he has no experience with this and he wouldn't know what to do or say. I'm sure he's mentally blocked any thoughts that I might someday have sex."

Cody found that hard to believe, but kept his mouth shut. "Then let's not traumatize the poor guy." He drew her close. "One kiss and I'm leaving. It'll be dawn before you know it."

"And I'll see you at the ranch."

"Yeah, I hadn't given that much thought. I'll need to be careful. My family is way too observant and I tend to show what I'm feeling."

"But you'll be busy getting ready for your trip. You won't be around much."

"I'd expected to be busy, but if I take Bert, that's one big issue solved. Buying a horse, or even finding the right one to rent, was going to take time."

She wound her arms around his neck and gazed up at him. "What about a trailer? I know you don't want that big one the ranch has."

"I'll buy one. Zane gave me a couple of leads to check out. I can do that tomorrow."

"So looking for trailers takes care of one day. What else?"

"Not much. Make sure my camera's in working order, buy food. Theoretically, once I find the right trailer, I could leave soon after that."

"Oh." She packed a lot of disappointment into that one syllable.

His heart squeezed. "I'm picky about trailers, though. I have a feeling I won't find the right one for quite a while. Could take me at least ten or twelve days of looking."

"You'd stall on the trailer because of me?"

"You sound surprised." He slipped his hand under her jacket and rubbed the small of her back. Clearly she wasn't used to people accommodating her needs.

"But aren't you eager to start your trip? Kendra said you've been planning it since high school."

"I'm very eager to start the trip, but I'm not a fool." He wished he could see her expression and she could see his, but they'd moved away from the light. "If a hot woman makes a special request, I'm more than happy to wait a few days."

"That's gracious of you, but I don't want to hold up the adventure you've dreamed of for ten years."

He smiled. "Trying to get rid of me?"

"Of course not, but your trip is important."

"So is spending time with you."

She hesitated, as if marshaling more arguments.

"I want to stay," he murmured. "Can you accept that?"

She took a deep breath. "Yes, okay. But I'm honored, Cody. Truly, I am."

"I'm the one who's honored." Tipping his head to avoid hitting her with the brim of his hat, he leaned down and touched his mouth to hers.

With a little whimper, she pulled him into a deeper kiss and in no time tongues were involved.

He hadn't meant to let that happen, but she was turning into a very good kisser. She'd also learned to rub against him until she got the effect he knew she was going for, a bulge in his jeans. He lifted his mouth a fraction from hers. "Stop that."

"I like seducing you."

"I can tell. But this isn't the time or the place."

"Are you crazy with lust?"

"Yes."

"Good. Me, too." She wiggled out of his arms. "See you tomorrow."

"Don't be offended if I avoid you like the plague."

"You can't be obvious about it. That will look suspicious."

"Then I'll make damned sure we're never alone." He had visions of backing her into a vacant stall and tossing her down on a bed of straw.

"Oh, for heaven's sake. It's not like I'll be prancing around in a tank top and sleep shorts. I'll look like I always do. You'll be able to resist me." She backed out of the shadows and moonlight fell on her unbound hair.

He was mesmerized. "Don't be so sure."

"Goodnight, Cody."

"Goodnight, Faith." He watched until she slipped through the front door. Then he walked around back and waited until a light came on in her room. If she hadn't left the light on when she'd fallen asleep, he wouldn't have known which room was hers.

She came to the window and looked out. He waved and she waved back. Then she took off her jacket. He stood gazing at her like a lovesick schoolboy, still not quite believing that this was the same woman who came to work every day in baggy jeans and oversized shirts.

Maybe the disguise had been on purpose. Dressed like a man, she wouldn't attract male attention. She and her dad could live their quiet, asexual life and not be troubled by unwanted complications. She still planned to live that way, once she'd had her fling.

She took hold of the hem of her tank top. *No, she wouldn't*. Two hours ago, she'd been an untouched virgin. Surely she wouldn't.... He groaned as she pulled the tank top over her head and tossed it away. A quick shimmy of her hips and the shorts were gone. She stood in front of the window and allowed him to look his fill.

He couldn't have moved if an angry bull had been bearing down on him. He scarcely blinked. His cock strained against his fly. Then she blew him a kiss and closed the curtains. He stared at the window in disbelief. Had that really happened?

Unless he'd started hallucinating, something he'd never done in his life, Faith had just treated him to a fantasy. He couldn't call it a strip tease because she'd made no attempt to draw out the process. She'd simply stood in front of the window and taken off her clothes. For him.

If she'd wanted to give him a visual that would stay with him for hours, days...hell, maybe forever...she'd succeeded. After several long, slow breaths, he managed to walk around the house and back down the road to his truck. But he was deaf to the night sounds and blind to the stars shining through the trees. He saw only Faith, her glorious hair falling over her shoulders and curling around her creamy breasts as she stood proudly in front of her window.

He was the luckiest SOB in the universe and she thought he was doing her a favor. She'd thrown in the loan of her horse to sweeten the deal in case making love to her turned out to be boring. There was nothing boring about that woman. If he expected to keep her interested, he'd have to ramp up his game.

The candles had been a good idea, though. He'd blown them out before walking her home, although the rain earlier had assured him nothing would catch on fire.

After gathering all the glass candle holders, he tucked them in their original boxes and shoved them behind the pillows like before. Same with the package of condoms.

He would have been happy to use another one tonight, but that would have been a mistake. She was getting the hang of this seduction business, but her body was still new to the physical connection. Although his experience with virgins was limited, he had a fair amount of common sense. She might think she was ready for pedal to the metal sex, but she wasn't. He'd promised not to hurt her and he'd keep that promise.

Driving home, he thought about what the next several days would bring, and the next several nights. He'd agreed to Faith's plan because who could reject a woman who'd used vanilla as an aphrodisiac? But he hadn't considered the consequences.

He was the most transparent guy she'd ever meet, which made him a bad candidate for a secret affair. She'd wanted trustworthy, which he was, but he didn't know how to be devious. He'd already messed up while buying the condoms and the candles. Both Aunt Jo and Ellie Mae knew he was up to something. Zane was on the trail, too.

Nobody had guessed who he was conspiring with, but it wouldn't take Aunt Jo long to figure that out. Zane would, too, since he had so much opportunity to observe the two of them together. He'd notice if Cody started avoiding her.

He parked next to the house and climbed out of the truck. If he had his druthers, he'd sleep in the camper surrounded by memories of Faith. He'd have a tough time explaining that, so he crept carefully into the house and went back to his bedroom.

But he couldn't take off his clothes without remembering how Faith had taken off hers—twice. She'd been just as willing to strip in the camper as in her bedroom. She covered up for the rest of the world, but she hadn't hesitated to reveal everything to him.

That was humbling. She'd met him briefly the day she was hired, and in those few minutes she'd felt a visceral connection that had told her he was the one to give her this ultimate experience. After making that commitment, she was all in, at least until everything ended when he left.

He was touched by her calm acceptance of his departure and her life in general. It wasn't his place to question that, especially when he wasn't sticking around. He could, however, do his level best to give her the one thing she'd asked for. Well, she wasn't the only one who wanted it, now. He wanted it for her, and he'd be her partner in wringing every ounce of pleasure out of the next two weeks.

* * *

The next morning Faith dressed in the clothes she always wore to work, but they didn't feel quite right today. They were comfortable and allowed her freedom of movement, but they were too big. She'd bought them that way for years. The loose fit had never bothered her before.

But Cody had said she was a hot woman. Hot women didn't wear clothes that were too big. On the other hand, Cody would be gone in less than two weeks, along with his opinion that she was hot. She'd asked him to have sex with her so she could find out what it was like, not so she could rethink her wardrobe. If she changed anything, her dad would notice and ask what was going on.

Her internal argument continued as she drove down Wagon Wheel Lane and passed the spot where Everything Had Changed. She thought of it that way, like the title of a book. Before Cody had thrown stones at her window, she'd been one person. She wasn't the same person this morning. No point in pretending she was.

She arrived in time to help feed. Zane was there but not Cody, which was probably a good thing. She didn't mention him, but Zane did. He said Cody had found a faulty latch on his camper shell and had taken it back to the dealer first thing this morning to get it repaired before the shop got busy.

Zane had no reason to tell her that, so her paranoid brain wondered if he'd said it to see if she'd react. She didn't. Zane couldn't possibly have information about what had happened last night on Wagon Wheel Lane. Yet she couldn't shake the idea that people would look at her and *they would know.*

By mid-morning she'd convinced herself that was ridiculous. But when Mandy showed up to spend an hour working with Licorice, Faith studied her outfit. The jeans weren't fancy. They didn't have bling on them or even embroidery. But they fit like a dream. Anyone looking at Mandy in those jeans would know she was a hot woman.

Mandy's shirt was the same story. It was even plaid like Faith's, but the cut was completely different. The shirt hugged her torso and emphasized her breasts. Even when she tucked her hair under her hat, which she often did, she looked sexy.

After they finished their session with Licorice and turned her out to pasture, they walked back to the house to have a cup of coffee with Kendra. Faith worked up her courage to ask about Mandy's jeans. "Did you get them here?" She was hoping they were from a store in Bozeman, or maybe Billings. She'd make the drive, especially if she could find a sale.

"I bought them in New York." Mandy brushed a piece of straw off her leg. "But I had to alter them because they didn't fit the way I wanted."

Faith sighed. "I was afraid of that, but I'm not surprised. Everything you wear fits you perfectly."

"Thank you." Mandy glanced over at her. "Are you looking for a nice pair of jeans?"

"I wouldn't mind, although I don't have a lot to spend." Faith was out of her depth, but she soldiered on. Girl talk wasn't her specialty. "I mean, the ones I have are good quality. They're just a little...big."

"Finding jeans that fit exactly right is so tough. We're all built differently. If I hadn't learned how to use a sewing machine, I'd be screwed."

"Unfortunately, I don't sew."

"But I do. Maybe I can help."

"Oh, Mandy, I couldn't ask you to—"

"Why not? It's fun for me. Would you let me take a couple pairs of your jeans and see what I could do with them?"

"What would you charge?"

"Not a thing. Like I said, it's fun. But if you insist on doing something in return, you can teach me that cool rope trick you showed me the other day."

"Deal." She hesitated. "If it's not too much trouble, could you look at my shirts, too?"

"Oh, shirts are my specialty! Bring 'em on."

Faith shook her head in wonder. "I've never known anyone who was so thrilled about messing with clothes."

"You do, now. I'll take your measurements while we have coffee with Aunt Kendra. I know she has a tape measure because I gave her one. Then bring me your stuff tomorrow and I'll get started."

"Thank you. That would be awesome." Mandy's eagerness mystified her, but the prospect of having at least two outfits that fit was exciting. She couldn't wait for Cody to see her in them. She wished they could be finished by tonight, but she'd have to go on their ride in her baggy clothes. She had nothing else.

8

Cody had taken a page out of Faith's playbook and manufactured a problem with his camper shell that didn't exist. He hoped he wasn't getting good at telling lies, but this one had rolled right off his tongue when he was talking to his mom and Zane first thing this morning. Consequently he'd left the ranch before Faith had arrived. She'd appreciate that and so did he.

He'd treated himself to breakfast at the Eagles Nest Diner and then browsed the camping aisle in the hardware store. He found a Coleman stove on sale and some cookware and utensils, so he'd checked off most of the items on his list. The horse trailer was the only major thing left.

Then he noticed the camping mattresses. He'd looked at them the previous day and had rejected them as unnecessary for his trip. While he'd have some luxury whenever he returned to his truck, he wanted to rough it out in the wilderness. Even the tent seemed like overkill, except that he didn't relish sleeping with a rattlesnake and getting bit when he was miles from civilization.

The camping mattress wouldn't be for his trip, but one of them, or better yet two, would add immeasurably to the experience with Faith this evening. They were thin enough to roll up and tie behind the saddle, but they also self-inflated once the valve was open. They'd provide decent cushioning for that thrusting action she was looking forward to.

Focusing on that had a self-inflating effect on him, so he walked the aisles some more and wondered how in hell to get two camping mattresses past Faith's dad. Then he had it. He needed to take his saddle tonight and make sure it fit Bert.

He'd put his saddle and both mattresses in the back of his truck and drive down to the barn when he arrived instead of stopping in front of the house. Unless Faith's dad followed them to the barn—could happen but hopefully not—they'd saddle the horses and transfer the mattresses without Jim being the wiser.

As it was he didn't know how Faith had planned to smuggle a blanket along on their ride. She'd probably intended to tie a bedroll behind her saddle and make sure they didn't ride past the front porch on their way out. Or she might have thought they could make do with a couple of saddle blankets. He could imagine that if they were desperate. Yesterday he wouldn't have agreed to such primitive conditions, but today was a different story.

He bought two camping mattresses. He'd take them back to the ranch after the ride along with his saddle. Being in possession of those mattresses wouldn't raise any eyebrows at home. He was loading up with camping equipment and he could easily explain them.

By now it was nearly noon and time for his appointment with Steve, one of the leads Zane had given him on a used horse trailer. Cody had contacted the guy and offered to pick up a couple of burgers on the way over to the construction site where Steve worked. They could talk during Steve's lunch hour and he'd promised to bring the trailer to the site.

Cody made a quick trip to the Burger Barn, the closest thing to fast food in Eagles Nest. The food didn't come out very fast, but Burger Barn had a drive-through, which gave the appearance of efficiency. Most people didn't use the drive-through because even with two or three vehicles waiting, a customer could sit in line for thirty minutes. Cody phoned his order in ahead and got to the construction site right on time.

A new feed store was going in and the trailer was sitting in a parking area next to the building site. The freshly washed silver exterior sparkled in the midday sun. It would look perfect gliding along behind his truck. But it was a double. Steve must have failed to mention the capacity to Zane.

In between bites of his burger, Steve apologized about the misunderstanding. "I thought people would be happy to get a bigger one for less money." He leaned against the side of the trailer, which he'd obviously detailed. It was immaculate.

"Most people don't have just the one horse. Horses get lonely, you know, just like people."

"I do know." Cody liked Steve, a bearded guy who looked to be in his thirties. What a shame the trailer was a double. "This is a special situation because I'm taking off for two months of wilderness exploration. It's just me, so I only need one horse and a single trailer."

"Sounds like a cool idea. If it was me, though, I'd want to take my girlfriend. That kind of thing is more fun if you can share it, you know?"

"It can be, I guess. I just always figured on doing this by myself. Been planning it for years."

"Oh, well, that's different. It's like a quest, then."

"You could call it that."

Steve nodded and stroked his beard. "I'd still take my girlfriend, even on a quest. But then again, she's easy to be with, doesn't insist on five-star accommodations. We've taken this trailer and our horses on plenty of campouts and we always have a great time."

"Then why are you selling it?"

"We're having twins, so we decided to get married. She can't ride until after the kids are born, and we're planning to get a couple more horses so I have my eye on a four-horse trailer."

"Congratulations on those twins." Cody offered his hand. "I have two older brothers who are twins. Makes for an interesting dynamic."

"Do they look something like you?"

"Sort of. Why?"

"I'll bet those are the ol' boys who used to work at the Guzzling Grizzly."

"Yep. Trevor tended bar and Bryce waited tables. You know them?"

"Just from the Guzzling Grizzly. Asked about them the other night and the owner said they were in Texas working for some big outfit down there."

"They are and it's good money, but they're getting homesick. I expect they'll be back working at the bar come September."

"That'll be too late for the wedding. I'd planned to ask Bryce to play guitar for it. He has a nice sound and a good voice, but they said he'd given it up completely."

"He has." And a wedding gig would be the worst kind of torture for Bryce.

"That's a shame," Steve said. "He was good. Anyway, I can understand them wanting to come home even if they can't make the same money here. Personally, I wouldn't live anywhere else." His phone chimed. "Well, time to get back to the job. Nice talking to you."

"Same here." Cody tipped his hat. "Good luck selling the trailer."

"Wish I could sell it to you. It would go great with that truck of yours."

"It would. Just not the right size."

Although Cody had another trailer to look at, he decided to put it off and go back to the ranch. He'd meant to stay away for the entire day, but the truth of it was, he missed Faith. He missed her gap-toothed smile and the sprinkling of freckles over her cute little nose.

In less than two weeks he wouldn't be able to simply drive a few miles and be back in her space, but he could do that now and forgoing the pleasure seemed stupid. But he also wanted to slow play the trailer search. Once he bought one, his mom and Zane would know he didn't have anything keeping him in Eagles Nest.

Saying he had to get used to riding Bert wouldn't hold any water with them. The chestnut gelding had been Faith's horse for years and she was an excellent trainer. Getting acquainted with Bert would take one or two rides, tops. Had Faith thought of how fishy their nightly outings would look to everyone, including her dad?

The trailer, though, was a physical barrier to leaving, so he'd work that excuse for as long as possible. Maybe he should fall in love with one that needed major renovation. Too bad he hadn't said anything like that to Zane. Instead he'd told his brother the exact opposite—that he wanted a used trailer in tip-top shape.

He'd embellished that statement by adding that he'd rather spend the money than use up precious time getting a fixer-upper road-worthy. And Faith had offered him a free horse so he couldn't suddenly act like he was watching his budget without raising suspicion. Delaying his departure would be a tricky maneuver.

The dirt road leading to the ranch had dried in the warmth of the sun, which gave him hope that the clearing Faith had chosen for their next sexual experiment would be dry, too. When the ranch was in sight, he drove past the arena and glanced over to see if she was there.

She was, and the sight of her made him happy. There was no mistaking those baggy clothes, but he knew what was under them, now. He was the only person who did other than Faith herself, and she hadn't appreciated the beauty of her body. Maybe she did, now.

She perched on the rail on the far side of the arena while she gave a riding lesson. His mom sat on a folding chair outside the enclosure near the gate. She leaned forward, like she was itching to be in there, too. By the time he got back from his journey, she might be.

He was glad he'd asked his mom whether they'd keep Faith on after the emergency was past, but he hadn't asked her if Faith knew she had a permanent position. Parking his truck by the barn so he could load his saddle easily later, he walked over to the arena. Maybe he'd ask now.

His mom glanced at him and smiled. "I don't see a trailer hitched to your truck."

"I looked at a beauty. Great price, but it was a double."

"That's too bad. You only looked at one?"

"That's all. I spent a lot of time browsing the camping aisle at the hardware store. Found a bargain on a Coleman stove."

"Is the latch on your camper fixed?"

"What...oh, yeah. It's fine." He'd come damn close to asking what latch she was talking about. He'd never make it as an international spy. Crouching next to her, he gazed across the arena at

Faith, who'd climbed down to adjust the position of the rider's feet in the stirrups. "Who's the student up on Strawberry?"

"Believe it or not, that's Deidre."

"You're kidding." He'd known Deidre all his life but he hadn't recognized her in boot cut jeans, a Western shirt and a riding helmet. He was used to seeing her in the fashionable outfits she wore when she was selling real estate or the colorful leisure outfits she wore when she was hanging out with his mom.

Deidre and two other women, Christine and Judy, had been in his mom's high school graduating class. They'd all stayed in town and had remained close friends, forming what they called the Whine and Cheese Club. They'd insisted for years that his mom was the only one with the riding gene. "What got her out here?"

"I think it was the idea of having Faith teach her instead of me or even Zane."

"That's crazy."

"Not really, if you think about it. She admitted that it's hard to be a beginner in front of someone you've known forever, or worse yet, the son of somebody you've known forever. At least it is for her. She's very competitive."

"Then should you even be sitting here?"

"We talked about it and she likes having me watch from a distance but I've been instructed to keep my mouth shut."

Cody grinned. "How's that working out for you?"

"I've ground all the enamel off my back molars."

"You don't think Faith's doing it right?"

"Oh, she's doing it perfectly. I just keep wanting to add my two cents."

"I'm so surprised." Cody gazed at Deidre as she started around the arena, her movements tentative. That was so unlike the woman he knew, so maybe she did need a relative stranger like Faith to guide her. He hadn't put it together until now, but without Deidre, he might never have met Faith.

Two months ago, when his mom broke her leg, Deidre happened to be selling a nice little place on Wagon Wheel Lane to Jim Underwood. Faith had asked Deidre if any ranches in the area needed a good hand and Deidre had told Zane and his mom that Faith looked like an excellent candidate to fill in while his mom recuperated.

He'd forgotten how Faith had come to be here, but Deidre was the link. If Jim had chosen a different real estate agent...but he hadn't. As a result, his daughter was no longer a virgin. Cody would keep that secret safe in his heart. A surge of protectiveness warmed him.

He glanced up at his mom, whose jaw was tight from keeping her comments to herself. "Does Faith know her job is secure?"

"Yes. I've told her."

"Good. I forgot to ask that before."

"I was serious about inviting her and her dad over to dinner. How does tomorrow night sound?"

"Great." He couldn't respond any other way, but the idea curdled his blood. What a nightmare, after what he and Faith had done last night and what they planned to do tonight. Meeting Jim before the action had taken place had been awkward, but now? Cody wouldn't be able to look the man in the eye.

"Why don't you want to?"

"I want to."

"No, you don't. I recognize that tone of voice when you say *great.* You'd rather have a root canal."

He scrambled to supply a reason for his negative reaction. "He's a nice guy, but I'm not sure he did right by Faith, raising her in a bunkhouse."

"I doubt he had a lot of options. Besides, she loved that time in her life."

"I can see why she would, but she also missed out on a lot."

"So did you."

"What?" He turned to stare at her.

"After your father died, well-meaning people advised me to make a greater effort to expose my boys to male role models. They even suggested I was shirking my responsibility by not remarrying as soon as possible."

"That's crap."

"I thought so, too, but it's true that you didn't have a strong male role model in your life."

"No, I had you. I had your girlfriends from high school. I had Aunt Jo. I'll take that setup over some bogus replacement dad."

She smiled. "Thank you. But do you see my point? He did the best he could under difficult circumstances. Most of us do."

"You're right." He gazed at her. "But then, you usually are."

"That's why they pay me the big bucks."

9

Faith forced herself to concentrate on Deidre's lesson, but it wasn't easy after Cody arrived. She was glad to see him and she'd missed him like the devil, but knowing he was over there talking to Kendra was beyond distracting.

Deidre must have noticed her preoccupation, because she pulled up to where Faith sat on the rail. "I don't blame you," she said in a stage whisper. "He's a cutie-pie."

"I guess."

"Oh, honey, there's no guesswork involved. We've all been in love with Cody McGavin since he was six months old. You should get Kendra to show you the picture of Cody on a furry rug at that age. We all predicted he'd grow up to be a beautiful man and we were right."

Faith hoped Deidre hadn't noticed her pink cheeks. "Do you want to take one more circuit around the arena?"

"Yes, yes, I do. Thank you for being so patient with me. I'm going to conquer this. I've envied Kendra for years because she could ride."

"You'll catch on in no time."

"I will, because I'm awesome, and don't you forget it."

Faith laughed. "I won't." She'd liked Deidre since the day they'd met. Thanks to Deidre, she'd been hired at Wild Creek Ranch and had been swept up in the lives of Kendra, Zane and Mandy. Jo wasn't officially a McGavin but it felt like she was. Then there was Cody.

When he'd driven in this afternoon she'd noticed that he wasn't pulling a trailer and she'd smiled. He'd meant what he'd said about taking his time buying one. She cherished that about him. Cody meant what he said, and so did she.

That was important in a friendship, and that was ultimately what she was going for. She would make the most of this time and she believed he would, too. For her it would be everything, even if for him it would only be a chapter, an episode, a bright spot. That was okay. She was content to be a temporary bright spot in the life of Cody McGavin.

"Faith?"

She glanced up. Deidre looked amused as she sat astride the roan gelding. Strawberry just looked bored. Faith had no idea how much time had passed. "Did you go all the way around the arena?"

"Twice. And I'll have you know my seat was perfect."

"I'm sure it was. Listen, I promise I'll be more focused next time."

"Honey, you don't have to explain anything to me. If he weren't my dear friend's son, I'd go for him myself. I can cougar it up with the best of them. But McGavin blue is off-limits for this woman."

"Excuse me?"

"It became a thing when they were in school. They're as different as can be, but they all have those eyes. It became known as McGavin blue."

"I've only met two of them, but I can see what you mean about the eyes."

"Three. You've met three."

"Who's the third?"

"Kendra."

"Oh, of course."

"So how do I get off this beast without embarrassing myself? I've lost all feeling in my feet."

"I should have brought the mounting block. Hang on." She hopped down. "Hey, Cody, Deidre needs assistance. Would you kindly show her how a gentleman helps a lady down from her horse?"

"Sure thing." He stood and climbed over the rail. "Hey, Deidre."

"Hey, yourself, Cody. You're looking good."

"You, too." He crossed the arena. "Like you were born to the saddle."

"More like welded to the saddle."

He nudged back his hat and gazed up at her. "It's great to see you out here. Before you know it, you'll be moseying down the trail with Mom."

"That's the plan. By the time she's cleared to ride, I can go along without crippling myself. It should work. Faith is a wonderful teacher."

"Thank you." Faith's cheeks heated. She hadn't been very attentive towards the end but she'd been dealing with a major distraction.

"I'm sure she is." Cody gave her a warm glance.

McGavin blue, indeed. When she met his gaze, images from last night came flooding back and her heart raced. She'd thought maintaining a breezy attitude with him would be easy when other people were around. Boy, had she been wrong.

Fortunately, he turned his attention back to Deidre. "Let's get you down from that animal. Put one hand on the saddle horn and the other on the pommel. Then take your right foot out of the stirrup and swing it over Strawberry's rump. I'll hold onto you so you won't fall."

"Are you sure about this? I'm not a lightweight like your mother. You might drop me."

"No worries." He grinned. "We have insurance." He grasped her around the waist and guided her gently from the saddle to the ground. Then he made sure she was steady on her feet before he let go.

"Thank you, Cody." She turned and smiled at him. "But now you've spoiled me. I'm afraid you'll need to stick around a few more weeks so you can help me down after every lesson. You're okay with that, right?"

"Absolutely. I'm here to serve."

Faith knew they were kidding around, but the thought of having him stay for several weeks tantalized her. It would never work, though. She could manage an affair for a couple weeks without her dad finding out, but any longer than that and he'd know. So would everyone else.

Or maybe she'd just blown it. If Kendra had noticed her staring at Cody when she was supposed to be watching Deidre circle the arena, that would be a clue. Or maybe not. Deidre said women routinely stared at him, so Kendra might be used to it by now.

Cody opened the gate and Deidre led Strawberry through. Teaching a student how to handle a horse whether riding or walking back to the barn was important to Faith. Next lesson she'd show Deidre how to saddle and bridle the gelding.

Kendra stood and balanced on her walking cast. "You did great, Dee."

Deidre laughed. "And you kept your mouth shut like you promised. I'm impressed, girlfriend."

"Wasn't easy considering I'm such a buttinski." She glanced at Faith. "You did a fabulous job."

"Thank you."

"Listen, I was just suggesting to Cody that it would be fun if you and your dad came to dinner tomorrow night. Do you think you can make it?"

Yikes. Instinctively she wanted to look at Cody but she managed not to. Kendra was unknowingly taking away one of their precious nights together, but the invitation was a generous idea. "That sounds wonderful," she made herself say. "I'll check with my dad, but he should be available." He would be. He was a guy without plans. She was the one with plans that would have to be scratched.

"I hope so." Kendra turned to Deidre. "Could you come, too? You were the magician who made all this happen. I don't know what we would have done without Faith the past two months."

"I'd love to come."

"Good." Kendra sounded pleased. "Which reminds me. Cody, will you be here for supper tonight?"

"Yes, but I'll be late. I'll help feed, and then I'm going out to Faith's house so I can take Bert for a test drive."

Faith was impressed with the casual way he said it.

"That's fine." Kendra gave his arm a pat. "I'll go ahead and eat, then. You can warm yours when you get home. Oh, and one of you needs to ask Jim if he can come to dinner tomorrow night. Don't forget."

"We won't." Faith and Cody said it in unison.

Kendra smiled at them. "That's cute. Now if you'll all excuse me, I have email to catch up on. The weekend trail rides are almost full, which makes me very happy. See you tomorrow night, Dee." She hobbled toward the house.

"I'll be there with bells on!" Deidre watched Kendra make her way up to the porch. "She's doing great."

"She certainly is." Faith admired Kendra's spirited recovery more than she could say.

"So what's next?" Deidre returned her attention to Faith. "Do we need to take everything off this horse and hose him down or something?"

"No hosing down today, but we'll remove his tack and give him a good grooming."

"I'll leave you two ladies to it," Cody said. "I need to fetch my saddle and put it in the truck for our ride tonight."

"Sounds good." Faith didn't dare look at him. As she and Deidre made their way over to the hitching post with Strawberry, she talked about the great progress Deidre had made instead of watching Cody load his saddle into the truck. Thankfully once he'd accomplished that he went up to the house.

But an hour later, after Deidre had left, Faith was in the middle of sweeping the tack room floor when Cody walked in. She stopped sweeping as her heart launched into overdrive. "I thought you didn't want to be alone with me."

He came toward her. "Being alone with you is all I can think about."

"But we can't—"

"I know, I know. I just wanted to apologize for the dinner thing." Although he looked like he wanted to kiss her, he paused and stuck his thumbs in his belt loops. "Mom brought it up while we were watching the lesson and I couldn't do anything except go along with it."

"Of course you couldn't. My dad might be happy about going or he might not want to. Ever since his accident he's been a different person. He used to sit around with the other ranch hands, playing poker and drinking beer. He was a social guy. But he says he's through with that life."

"All we can do is ask and let the chips fall." He glanced at the broom in her hand. "I interrupted your work. Let me help."

"Thanks, but I—"

"Cowboys like to help pretty ladies." He walked over and took the dustpan and whiskbroom from a shelf. "It's part of our DNA."

"I'm not pretty dressed like this."

"You're right." He used the whiskbroom to sweep the pile of dirt and straw she'd collected into the dustpan.

"Hey, you aren't supposed to agree with me."

He dumped the contents into a trash barrel and set the whiskbroom and dustpan beside it. "You're not pretty." His voice roughened and he turned toward her. "You're beautiful."

She met his gaze and her breath caught.

"I don't know how I missed seeing it that first day, but you're a stunner." He came toward her, desire burning in his eyes.

She loved hearing him say such things but she knew what was going on. "You're addlepated with lust."

"That's part of it, but you really are gorgeous. Your cheeks are so soft."

"Freckled."

"That makes you look more interesting. And your smile is magic."

"I have a space between my front teeth."

"Again, more interesting. You're fascinating to look at."

"Especially without my clothes."

"Okay, let the record show that you sent the discussion in that direction. I was only referring to the area above your neck. But now that you mention it, you blew me away last night when you posed in front of your window buck naked. That was bold, lady."

"You were just standing there, so I thought I should give you something to look at."

"You certainly did. I'll never forget it."

"Never? That's a long time." But she hoped he would remember.

"Never *is* a long time. But that was a spectacular view." He swallowed. "I want to kiss you so much."

She had trouble breathing. "Just kiss me?"

"For starters. All over your freckled body."

"Cody, I'm getting juicy again."

"And I'm getting hard. We need to stop this."

"How?"

He heaved a sigh. "We should talk about something else."

"Or you could go back to the house."

"That's just it. I don't want to. I like being with you." He tugged on the brim of his hat. "And by the way, I bought two camping mattresses for tonight. Can we take them out there without your dad seeing them?"

"You really are worried about doing it on the ground, aren't you?"

"Yes, damn it! It's not as much fun."

"You'd know better than I would." Thinking about him with another woman was a real buzzkill. But if he hadn't gained some sexual experience, he wouldn't be so knowledgeable on the subject. She liked that he was. She only had to stop picturing how he got that way.

"What do you think?" He gazed at her. "Can we smuggle the mattresses out there or not?"

"We can if my dad doesn't come down to the barn with us. I wasn't going to ride past the porch on our way to the clearing, because I planned to take a blanket."

"These will feel good under the blanket."

"You really think we'll need them?"

"I might not, but you will if you want thrusting to be going on. You'll be the one lying on the ground."

"Oh. Good point. Look, I'm two seconds away from jumping you, so please head on up to the house, okay? I'm getting really frustrated. I didn't used to understand this feeling but now I do."

"Are you sorry about that?"

She wrapped her free hand around the back of his neck. Then she kissed him hard on the mouth and knocked both their hats off. "I'm not sorry. Now git." She made a shooing motion with the broom.

"Yes, ma'am." Smiling, he picked up his hat and left the tack room.

10

Two hours later, Cody pulled in behind Faith in front of the cozy two-story frame house on Wagon Wheel Lane. They'd worked out their game plan after some debate. He hoped everything went smoothly.

Jim sat on the front porch as he had the first night. Last time he'd been working on a frayed bridle, but tonight he was sipping from a bottle of beer. Ever since meeting him, Cody had been trying to place who he looked like. Now it hit him—a younger version of Clint Eastwood.

He smiled when Cody and Faith got out of their respective trucks. "Evening, you two! Are you sure you don't have time to sit for a spell and have a beer?"

"Maybe next time, Dad." Faith went up the steps ahead of Cody. "Tonight we need to find out if Cody's saddle fits Bert and whether Cody likes riding him."

"Oh, you'll like Bert, son. But if for some reason the saddle doesn't fit right, you're welcome to try Ernie. He's built a little different."

"Thank you, sir. That's mighty generous of you considering you don't know me very well." Cody couldn't decide which startled him more—Jim's use of *son* or his offer of Ernie.

"I may not know you, but if Faith trusts you with her horse, that's good enough for me."

"I appreciate it. But I'm sure Bert will work out fine." Guilt gnawed at him as he thought about the evening's plans. He wished Jim wasn't being so damned nice.

If Cody were Faith's father, he wouldn't be pleased about this setup. He wouldn't want his daughter having her first sexual relationship with someone who was only in it for the short term and had the loan of a valuable horse as part of the deal. Viewed from that angle, Cody was making out like a bandit and Faith was getting the short end of the stick. Cody felt a little bit that way about it, too, which was why he had such difficulty interacting with Jim.

"By the way, Dad," Faith said, "Kendra asked if you and I could come to the ranch for dinner tomorrow night. She thought you'd like to see the place and finally meet her."

"That sounds nice, honey bun."

"It would be great if you could come," Cody said. "Mom puts on a great spread."

"Oh, and Deidre will probably be there," Faith added.

"Oh?" Jim blinked. "Are you talking about our real estate agent?"

"One and the same. I gave her a riding lesson today, her first ever, and Kendra asked her to come to dinner since without her, I wouldn't have the job at Wild Creek Ranch."

"Deidre doesn't ride?" Jim glanced at his daughter in obvious surprise. "Was she afraid?"

"Not that I can tell. She just never tried it, but she's ready to learn, now."

"Because of you," Cody said, gazing at Faith.

"Me?" She looked confused. "That makes no sense."

"It's true. I talked to Mom about it today. Deidre was too embarrassed to learn from Mom, who's one of her best friends. It's easier on her ego to take lessons from you."

"How funny. I had no idea that was the situation."

"But I get it," Jim said. "Deidre's a fireball. It must kill her to be bad at something."

Faith's attention swung immediately to her dad. "You think she's a fireball?"

"Don't you?"

"I do, but...anyway, never mind. Is that a yes? Can Cody tell his mom we'll be there?"

"It's fine with me, honey bun. I'd like to see where you work."

"Great," Cody said. "Then I guess Faith and I better get down to the barn and saddle up."

Jim lifted his beer. "Be careful."

Cody met his gaze. "We will, sir." He helped Faith into his truck.

The minute they started off she turned to him. "He thinks Deidre's a fireball? What's that about?"

"I have no idea, but he nailed her personality. She hates being bad at anything. Divorce was hard on her because she saw it as a failure. She's dated some guys since then, but Mom says Deidre won't remarry because she's terrified that she'll fail again."

"Then she's single. I thought so, but I wasn't certain. I mean, not that it matters."

Cody wasn't so sure. He'd seen Faith's reaction when her father had made a personal comment about Deidre. He'd been accurate, which meant he'd been paying attention. A man who paid attention usually had a reason. What an interesting development.

Turned out Cody's saddle fit Bert like a dream but he wasn't surprised. Ever since meeting Bert, he'd figured the tall chestnut would be making the journey with him.

They worked quickly to saddle up and tie a camping mattress behind each saddlebag. Cody took the blanket and added it to his bundle. Although Jim could wander down at any point in the preparations, his *be careful* comment indicated he planned to stay on the porch.

At last they were ready to mount up. Their bed wouldn't compare to what they'd enjoyed last night, but Cody was okay with that. He was glad the first night had been in a special setting with plenty of creature comforts. Tonight's venue would be more primitive, and maybe that was appropriate. He'd been having primitive urges all day.

The route she'd chosen allowed them to ride side-by-side, which was a bonus. She smiled at him. "This is a treat, being able to take them out together."

"Your dad won't even go on easy rides?"

"Nope. The horse that rolled on him was spooked by a piece of paper that blew across a very gentle trail. It was a freak accident that never should have happened."

"Maybe that makes it even scarier."

She sighed. "I think it does. His takeaway was that riding is unpredictable no matter what the circumstances."

"I'm glad he hasn't managed to transfer his fears to you."

"I was determined that wouldn't happen. I wish I could get him back on a horse, though. Having someone to ride with is fun." She looked over and gave him that endearing, gap-toothed grin. "How's Bert treating you?"

"He's a great horse. But I don't have to tell you that. You're doing me a huge favor."

"Backatcha. The clearing's just ahead."

"We're there already?"

"I didn't want to waste a lot of time riding around the countryside, so I picked a spot close to home."

She was so enthusiastic. A guy couldn't do much better than a good-hearted, beautiful woman who couldn't wait to get it on. He stood in his stirrups to survey the landscape and spied some cattle in the distance, but not a single critter was nearby. "Who owns the cattle?"

"There's a ranch not far from here. They have grazing rights on this land." She swung down.

"We can ground-tie those ol' boys. They're used to it."

"I'll bet they're not used to what we're about to do." He dismounted and dropped the reins to the ground. She'd cleared an area about the size of a queen bed. It was dry but not dusty yet. It would be in a couple of days, though.

"I hadn't thought of that." She took off her hat and hung it on the saddle horn. "Do you think we might spook them?"

"That depends." He followed her lead and left his hat on his saddle. Then he eliminated the distance between them and wrapped her in his arms. Ahh. This was what he'd been craving for hours. "How much noise are you planning to make?"

"I don't know." She snuggled against him. "How much did I make last night?"

"You hollered like a cowpoke on a Saturday night bender." Keeping one arm around her waist, he drew her braid over her shoulder, slipped the elastic off the end and tucked it in his pocket.

"Did not." She ran a finger along his jaw. "You shaved. When did you do that?"

"When you banished me to the house this afternoon."

"I'll bet you did that so you wouldn't scratch me when you kissed me and turned me into a puddle, hint, hint."

"I'm not going to kiss you, yet."

"Last night you unwound my braid and then you kissed me."

"Remembered that, did you?"

Her green eyes grew smoky. "I remember everything."

"So do I, and I'm not going to repeat myself and risk becoming boring. No wash, rinse, repeat for you, milady."

She laughed. "You're not going to let me forget that, are you?"

"No, ma'am. I intend to make you eat those words." He combed her hair with his fingers and let the tresses catch the golden light of the setting sun. Last night these silky strands had tickled his bare chest as she'd leaned over him, gasping from her climax.

Thanks to that memory and her sweet body pressed against him now, his cock was already hard and they hadn't untied the camping mattresses or the blanket. If he made the mistake of kissing her, they'd end up rolling in the dirt, the very thing he was trying to avoid.

"Guess I'll have to take matters into my own hands." She pulled his head down and pressed her mouth against his.

A gentleman didn't back away from something like that, especially when the lady in question turned a regular kiss into a French one. He couldn't believe that yesterday she hadn't known how to do such a thing and today she'd developed it into an art form.

In seconds, he was hotter than a campfire. Cupping the back of her head, he shifted the angle and took the kiss a notch deeper. He would get the mattresses, but first…

Oh, hey, now she was multitasking. While her tongue was turning him inside out, she'd unfastened enough snaps on his shirt to slide her hand inside and massage his pecs. He didn't know how she'd managed that, but damn. Good stuff.

Mattresses. He had to get the mattresses. He forced himself to stop kissing her. "We're not...we're not set up."

She gazed at him, her mouth wet and her breathing rapid. "I don't care."

"I do. Sort of." And he went back to kissing her because he couldn't stay away from those plump lips. Or the buttons of her shirt. He made a guess that her bra fastened in the back and he unhooked it to gain access.

Stroking her warm breasts made him groan with frustration and he broke the kiss again. "Listen, we have to—"

"The thing you did last night." She gulped for air. "Oral sex."

"I could do that." He saw where she was headed and he was hot enough that he wanted that for her. He could kneel in the dirt. It would work. He'd get the mattresses later.

"No, I mean, can *I*? Would you let me?" Her eyes gleamed.

He gazed at her in stupefied silence.

"It works both ways, right?" She dragged in a breath. "I mean, you must like it as much as I do."

He nodded, still unable to form actual words.

"Then can I?"

"Yes." The word came out as a harsh croak.

"Oh, good." She unbuckled his belt with trembling fingers. "You'll have to tell me how."

He swallowed. "You can't do it wrong."

"I could." She unfastened his zipper and shoved his jeans and briefs to his knees before stepping back. "Oh, my. I think it's bigger than before."

"Not possible."

"Maybe it's the light." She sank to her knees in front of him and lifted her head so she could look him in the eye. "How do I start?"

She'd given him many unforgettable moments in a very short time, but she'd have to work hard to top this one. She wanted instruction and he couldn't remember his name. He cleared his throat. "Wrap your hand around it." His voice sounded like a rusty hinge.

"How about both hands? There's plenty of room."

"Okay." As she did, he sucked in air and gritted his teeth. Erupting in her face would not be cool.

Immediately she let go. "See? I hurt you."

"Nope. Felt too good."

"Oh." Her frown of concern changed to a smile of triumph. "You're on the edge?"

"Mm-hm."

"Cool. Now what?"

"Take hold again." This time he was braced for it but he still thought it would be a very short lesson.

"And?"

He felt dizzy. He hoped he wouldn't pass out. "Lick, suck, whatever you want."

"Let me try that."

He quickly discovered he couldn't watch or he'd be toast. Instead he stared at the mountains and clenched his fists and his jaw while she did things with her mouth that she shouldn't know how to do. He didn't doubt that this was her first time. But she had instincts.

"Cody, you're panting."

"I know."

"And sweating."

"I know that, too."

"But are you having fun?"

"You have no idea."

"Me, too. Are you close?"

"Yes, ma'am."

"What happens then?"

"Either move aside...or swallow."

"You'll warn me?"

"Yep." As she went back to work, he began to shake. "Almost there. Almost...*now*." He choked back a roar of pleasure as release claimed him. He was working so hard not to yell and scare the horses that at first he didn't realize that she was still there. He heard her swallow. Then she licked away the drops of his orgasm.

He struggled to remain standing in the powerful aftermath. As if she knew he was about to collapse, she pulled up his briefs and his jeans. In moments, she'd tucked him back inside his clothes.

With a sigh of gratitude, he sank to his knees facing her. "You're the most amazing woman I've ever met."

She blushed. "I doubt that."

"Don't. You are, and I'm not saying it because I just had an incredible experience, which I did."

"Really? It wasn't lame?"

He smiled and cradled her face in both hands. "I can't picture you doing anything lame. You have such a zest for life. You're willing to try something you've never done before and risk screwing it up."

"I knew you'd forgive me if I did."

"Did you? Because it would make me happy if you trusted me that much."

"Like I said, I asked around. I knew you were beautiful, but when I found out you were also kind...search over."

"Lucky, lucky me." He kissed her gently and drew back. "You taste like sex."

"Is that okay?'

"It's more than okay. It's making me hard again."

"Good, because that oral action made me plenty juicy."

"You liked doing it, then?"

"Oh, yeah. I liked making you happy."

"You did."

"But I also have to admit that I went on a little power trip. It was awesome having the ability to make you quiver and moan. I'll bet if I practiced, I could get really good at it."

His brain went on tilt. “You can practice on me.”

“You’d let me?”

“I would.” Somehow he kept a straight face.

“That would be great.”

“You’re telling me.” He cleared his throat. “Ready to lay out the mattresses and blanket so we can try some thrusting and see how that goes?”

“Can’t wait.”

He couldn’t help it. He was grinning like a fool but she didn’t seem to take offense. He almost had been a complete fool. To think that two days ago, he’d decided to refuse her request. Thank God for vanilla.

11

Cody was looking at her as if he thought she was a goddess. Faith didn't object to that, but her outfit didn't feel particularly goddess-like. She helped him lay out the mattresses and link them together with the strap he'd bought. They put the blanket on top and finally had their horizontal surface in place.

Now she got his point about using more than a blanket. In a book, it sounded spontaneous and romantic. Maybe it would be on a grassy knoll in England. On a scraped-off piece of rangeland in Montana, a blanket spread on the ground might leave bruises on her backside and Cody's knees.

That's where his experience came in handy because he knew these things. But she continued to block any thoughts of him with other women. He had it easier, assuming he had similar issues with jealousy. He might not, but if he did, he had no one to be jealous of.

Considering the type of outfit she'd accepted as her uniform for most of her life, it was no wonder men hadn't asked her out. What man would be attracted to her when she was dressed that way? When Mandy had taken a tape measure to her this morning, Faith had been forced to think about why she'd chosen to wear clothes that were too big.

She hadn't had to search far for the answer. For most of her life, she'd wanted to be accepted by the cowhands at the ranches where she and her dad had worked. They'd been her extended family.

She'd copied their movements and their attitudes as she'd attempted to be as much like them as possible. But she'd grown up and developed curves. The only way to hide her blossoming figure had been with oversized clothes.

She might have dressed this way for the rest of her days except for three things—her dad's accident, a box of books, and a glimpse of Cody McGavin. Now that she had him here in the clearing she'd created for their sexual adventures, she wanted her baggy clothes off. She started stripping them away.

"Hey!" He caught her arm and pulled her close. "What's the rush?"

"I'd rather be naked."

"I'll vote for that, but if you don't mind, I'd like to peel them off myself."

"Why? I know you like me better without them."

"Last night I would have agreed with you. Today I don't."

She gazed at him in confusion. "There's nothing sexy about these clothes."

"There is when I know what they're disguising." He slid his hand under her unfastened bra. "Plain white cotton covers warm, satin skin and nipples like ripe raspberries. It's a secret you and I share but no one else knows. That gets me hot."

"I wouldn't have thought of the raspberry part." She arched into his hand, reveling in the way he touched her.

"That's my job, to look at you and think of raspberries." He brushed his thumb over her nipple. "Meanwhile no one else guesses what's hiding under baggy jeans and oversize shirts. I feel like a privileged insider. That's a turn-on."

She thought about Mandy's alterations. Guaranteed those clothes would turn him on more. "But you still want to get these off, right?"

"Yes, but slowly. I want to take time to enjoy each bit of sexy woman I uncover as I go."

"We didn't go slow last night." She snuggled closer, knowing how that affected him.

"That sleep outfit was unexpected. I went a little crazy when I saw you in that."

"Exactly." She wiggled out of his embrace and took off her shirt. "I like it when you go crazy."

Her move got the result she was looking for. He sucked in a breath when she shrugged out of her bra. Fire in his eyes, he started toward her.

"Hang on." She backed away from him. "I have to ditch my boots." She hopped on one foot and pulled off the first one.

He groaned as if in pain.

"Are you okay?" She hopped on the other foot to get the second boot off.

He gulped. "That hopping maneuver."

"What about it?"

"I almost came just watching you. You've taken jiggle to a whole new level." He crossed to her, swept her up in his arms and deposited her on the blanket. "You're right. Slow is overrated." He had her out of her jeans and panties in no time, partly because the jeans were so loose.

His clothes came off fast after that, too. He tossed his boots aside, flung off his shirt and shucked his jeans and briefs. But before he discarded the jeans, he pulled a condom out of the pocket and rolled it over his impressive erection.

Heart pounding in anticipation, she watched him. "I still can't believe that fits inside me."

"Barely. That's something we *are* gonna take slow." He moved over her and his gaze lingered on her breasts. "The light's fading, but I can still see your freckles."

She'd learned that when his eyes turned navy blue, he was becoming crazy with lust. "Ladies in olden days weren't supposed to have freckles."

"I'm glad we don't live in olden days. You're like a delicious pastry sprinkled with cinnamon." Braced on his forearms, he leaned down and placed kisses all over her breasts. "With a raspberry on top."

When he took one into his mouth and rolled it over his tongue, she felt the zing in a place that was becoming increasingly important to her. She wanted him there again, filling and stretching her, making her come. Cupping his butt cheeks, she tried to pull him down, but his muscles were rock hard. No wonder he looked so good in jeans.

He seemed enamored with her breasts, and what he was doing felt great, but she was impatient for the main event. She wrapped her legs around his and tugged again. "Cody, do it."

Lifting his head, he gazed into her eyes. "Once I start, I'll forget everything but being inside you."

"Fine with me."

"But you have such gorgeous breasts. And when you were taking off your boots..." His eyes glazed over and his breathing quickened. "Spectacular."

"You can love on them next time." Once again she was assuming they'd keep doing this, but his eyes were even darker, now, so she thought they would. "As long as you want."

"Mm." He kissed his way back to her mouth and brushed his lips over hers. "I like the way you think."

She pressed her fingertips into his backside. "You like the way I feel, too." She lifted her hips until she nudged the tip of his cock with her damp curls, but she couldn't get closer without some cooperation. "Remember how much you liked it last night when I was gradually sliding—"

"Heck, yeah." He stopped resisting her and sank partway in with a soft groan.

Oh, dear heaven, that felt amazing. She quivered with eagerness. "More."

"I don't want to hurt you." His voice had gone from mellow to husky.

There it was, the tightening she remembered. "I'll say something if you do." Then she decided to clarify. "I'll say *stop*. If I start babbling about anything else, assume it's all good."

"Remember that we can't spook the horses."

"I'll remember."

"I said it to remind me, not you." He eased in deeper.

Her first spasm hit.

His breath caught. "Faith?"

"*Thrust*, Cody."

He managed three strokes before she slapped a hand over her mouth to smother her cry as a climax rolled through her. He held very still as she gasped and trembled beneath him. As the lovely sensations gradually ebbed, she kept expecting him to come, too, just as he had the night before. But although he was breathing hard, he didn't have an orgasm.

When she'd dragged in enough air to ask him about it, he raised his head and smiled down at her. "That one was so quick, I thought you might like to go for another."

"Now?"

"Yes, ma'am."

"I couldn't."

"Are you sure?"

She checked in with her body. "I'm done."

"It's been known to happen if the guy can hold back."

"You held back so I could come twice?"

"Uh-huh."

"That's sweet, but...you go ahead."

"Then I will." He held her gaze as he drew back and slid in again. "Too much?"

"No. Everything feels easier, now."

"You're relaxed." He pushed in a little more, burying his cock to the hilt.

"Oh, I'm relaxed." She rested her hands on his firm buns and enjoyed the play of muscles as he kept up an easy rhythm.

"And juicy."

"That, too."

"Makes it nice for me." He drove in tight.

Oh. A wave of feeling rose from somewhere deeper, catching her by surprise.

He eased back and came in at a slightly different angle.

She swallowed. There it was again, stronger this time.

"Hey, Faith." His voice was roughened by passion. "What's going on, pretty lady?"

"I don't know, but—oh!" She dug her fingers into his butt as she rose to meet his next stroke. "I need to..."

"Come?"

"Maybe." She began to pant. "Can you go faster?"

"Sure can." His eyes were like midnight as he increased the pace.

The rapid friction drove her wild and the electric connection when he pushed home time after time after time built the waves of pleasure until they broke over her in a glorious deluge. At the last minute she put her hand over her mouth to muffle her wild cry. Moments later he shuddered against her, claiming his release with a low, triumphant groan.

As they lay crumpled together and gasping for breath she was the first to speak. "So I was wrong."

"Yeah."

"Thank you."

"Anytime."

She stroked his hair as he lay with his head on her shoulder. *Anytime*. It was what people often said when they'd been thanked for doing something. An automatic response. But in this case, it didn't fit. She wondered if he'd thought of that after he'd said it. Knowing Cody, he had.

He sighed and nestled closer. "It's getting chilly. We should go back."

"I'm not chilly." She closed her eyes and wrapped her arms around him.

"No, because you have a hot cowboy on top of you and an insulated camping mattress under you."

"I appreciate both."

"But which one do you appreciate more?"

"I don't know. Let me think."

"Hey. The answer is obvious."

"You're right. I appreciate the camping mattresses the most."

"Wrong answer."

"No, it's not. The hot cowboy went to the trouble and expense of getting them, which shows me how worried he was about exposing my tender body to the cold, hard ground. Whereas the hot cowboy is on top of me for a mostly self-serving reason."

"So you're beautiful and logical."

She smiled because at this very moment she could accept such extravagant praise. She was a woman who'd had two orgasms in a row. "Deal with it."

He chuckled. "Give a woman a couple of orgasms and she gets attitude."

"It's your own fault, then, isn't it?"

"Yes, and I—what was *that*?"

"What?"

"I think one of your horses just licked my ass."

She opened her eyes. "It isn't one of the horses."

"No?" He sounded a little freaked out. "Then what the hell is it?"

"A cow."

"Jesus Christ." Grabbing the base of the condom, he rolled away from her and scrambled to his feet. "Beat it!" He waved his free arm at the cow, who just stared at him with her big brown eyes and swished her tail.

He likely could use her help if she could only stop laughing. "You probably taste like salt."

"I don't care if I taste like a big slice of homemade apple pie!" He slapped the cow hard on the rump. "Move it, bossy! And take that sloppy tongue with you!"

The cow ambled off. Bert and Ernie watched her go and then went back to plucking what small blades of grass they'd been able to find in the clearing.

Cody glared at the departing cow. "And stay gone! If anybody's going to lick my ass, it sure as hell isn't going to be you!"

Faith sat on the blanket and enjoyed the show. "Are you into that? I'm a beginner, so you'll have to tell me these things."

Stalking back to the blanket, Cody fished a bandanna out of his jeans pocket and used it to whisk off the condom. Then he gazed at Faith. "You're welcome to put your tongue anywhere you want on this body. But a cow? I don't think so."

She struggled to keep her laughter under control. She'd never seen him lose his cool like that and she'd bet he hardly ever did. "I'm sorry. I swear that whenever I came out here, the cattle were far, far away."

"Except for the kinky one who likes to sneak up on unsuspecting men and lick their privates." But the dent had appeared in his cheek again, which meant he'd found his sense of humor.

"I'll take a guess that you'd like to find a different venue for next time."

"Good guess. I have a cozy camper. There must be a way we can enjoy it without anyone finding out."

"I'm sure there is. I'll think about it."

"Me, too."

She stood. "I feel bad, though, that you bought the camping mattresses and this might be the only time we use them."

"I don't feel the least bit bad about that." He wrapped an arm around her waist and pulled her close. "We had a cushioned bed where we discovered you're multi-orgasmic. That's worth a hundred camping mattresses."

"You discovered it." She cuddled against him, loving the skin-to-skin contact. "I had no clue, but you did. What made you think I was capable of that?"

"Easy. You've been super responsive ever since we started this adventure. You came three strokes into the first round. I had every reason to believe I could help you come again."

"It felt different from the other times."

"I think I've found your G-spot."

"My what?"

He tipped her chin up and kissed her gently. "If I explain that, we'll both get excited and climb back on that mattress to see if I can find it again. Then our kinky cow will show up and want in on the action. Let's postpone that discussion until we're naked and protected from cows."

"I imagined conducting this affair would be so easy."

He tucked her hair behind her ear. "It has been."

"No, it hasn't. It took more than I expected to get you to agree, and then it rained and you had to go to extra trouble."

"Worth it."

"Okay, I admit that turned out great, but when we finally follow my plan, the one I thought would be so uncomplicated, a cow licks your butt."

"Details. The important part, the connection between you and me, has been...perfect."

As the sun slipped below the horizon, she had just enough light to see into his eyes. She found sincerity and compassion there. And desire, an emotion she'd never shared with anyone except Cody. "It has been perfect." She gave him a long, slow kiss. Thanks to Cody, she'd discovered she was multi-orgasmic. That must make her a *really* hot woman.

12

Cody drove under the speed limit on the way home. He couldn't remember the last time he'd done that. The needle on his dash routinely sat five miles over, or on an open road with no cops in sight, a lot more.

All his life he'd been in a hurry—to start school, get his license, graduate, drink legally, land a job away from home, and finally take his big trip. But he was in no hurry to put an end to this special time with Faith. He felt as if they were building something solid, something he couldn't picture tearing down when he left at the end of next week.

She was thinking the exact opposite, though. He could see it in her eyes. She'd meant this to be temporary and she had a wrecking ball standing by. When the time was up, she'd deploy that sucker. Then again, she didn't have any experience with these things. She had no idea how much she'd miss him after they called it quits.

He'd had his share of painful breakups, and saying goodbye had never been easy. With Faith, though, he was looking at impossible. How could he walk away from someone who had him laughing one minute and hotter than a skillet of hash browns the next? If his trip marked the end of hanging out with her, he didn't want to go.

Yeah, there it was, the thing he hadn't wanted to admit. The more time he spent with her, the less excited he was about a trip he'd eagerly anticipated for years. That alone should tell him that something significant was going on between them.

She wouldn't want to hear it, though. Her neat little plan would collapse unless he left on schedule. She'd laid out exactly what she wanted—a brief, passionate interlude—so if he could forget about himself for five minutes and think about Faith, he'd give her that and blow out of town.

He'd managed to depress the hell out of himself by the time he parked next to the ranch house. He couldn't go in dragging his ass or his mom would ask what was wrong. In the past, he'd been able to tell her, but this time he couldn't. Damn.

Okay, he'd hit the shower before he spent any time talking with her. He could use one after all that activity topped off by cow slobber, and he'd have his happy face on by the time he came back out. When he breezed through the door, she was on the sofa reading. She glanced up.

He didn't give her a chance to say anything. "Hey, Mom! Gonna take a quick shower before I eat. See you in a few." He headed down the hall.

Fifteen minutes later, he emerged from his room prepped to tell her that Bert was an awesome horse and Faith's dad would be coming to dinner. She wasn't on the sofa anymore but he heard her moving around in the kitchen. He found her dishing out his dinner—meatloaf, mashed potatoes and gravy along with a side of green beans. His salad and an open bottle of beer already sat on the small kitchen table.

"Thank you. You didn't have to do that."

"I wanted to. Have a seat." She set his full plate on the table.

Her voice sounded funny, sort of choked up.

Instead of sitting down, he wrapped an arm around her shoulders. "Are you okay?"

"Yes." She sniffed.

Gently he turned her to face him. "No, you're not. You've been crying."

"Which is stupid! Ryker is fine!"

"Did you talk to him?"

"He called." She pulled a tissue out of her pocket and wiped her nose.

"Instead of the video chat? I thought he always—"

"He does do the video chat normally, so when he called, I got scared."

"Why did he call?"

She gave him a watery smile. "The real reason or the excuse he used?"

"Both."

"He *said* he called because he's decided to buy a small plane and subcontract with the commuter airline that's based outside of town. He wanted to make sure I wasn't counting on him to work at the ranch when he came back."

"Were you?"

"I was staying loose to see what happened. If he'd wanted to work here, I would have put him on the payroll, but I'd have to juggle the money because I'm determined to keep Faith."

"So in a way, his decision is a good thing."

She nodded. "If I had an emergency, like if Zane or Faith had some issue and couldn't be here, I'm sure he'd fill in. But I know how he loves to fly, so his plan is good for everybody."

"But you don't think that's why he called."

"No." She sniffed again. "We have a video chat scheduled for next week and he could have mentioned this then. I think he called because something bad happened and he needed to hear my voice."

"Oh, Mom." He gathered her close and mentally railed against his big brother for putting her through this. "Maybe that wasn't it."

"I'm pretty sure it was. When he was little and something scared or upset him, he'd stammer and trip over his words. Sometimes he still does that. He was doing it tonight."

"That means he's scared? I thought it meant he was mad."

"Oh, no. When Ryker's mad, his words come out like bullets from a machine gun and they're deadly accurate. That's assuming he's talking at all."

"I've seen him like that, too." He gently released her. "I thought it was different kinds of mad. I can't imagine him being scared of anything." He'd always been in awe of his oldest brother, who was built like a tank and had a commanding presence. Nobody messed with Ryker, which had come in handy on one memorable occasion. Cody had been a skinny runt at fourteen, no match for the three overgrown fools who'd thought he was easy pickings. But those three had been no match for Ryker.

"Don't tell him I pointed it out to you, okay?"

"I won't, but that's interesting. I thought he was mad when he had that fight with his girlfriend in the front yard. But he couldn't have been afraid of April. She never would have even slapped him, let alone done serious damage."

"He was probably afraid of losing her. She'd warned him that if he enlisted she'd break up with him. I think she hoped he'd change his mind."

"I could have told her he wouldn't."

His mom grimaced. "I did tell her. I knew they wouldn't make it."

"Does she know he's coming home in August?"

"I think everyone in Eagles Nest knows, but I didn't tell her personally. That would have been too pointed."

"Does he know she's back in town?"

"I certainly haven't mentioned it. He'd think I was hinting that he should look her up. I won't do that. I'm sure they've both grown and changed. A lot of water has gone under the bridge or over the dam or whatever the saying is."

He gazed at her. "The same was true for Zane and Mandy and look how that turned out."

"Ryker is not Zane. Now sit down and eat or my efforts to warm up your food will be wasted."

"Yes, ma'am." He pulled out a chair for her.

She smiled her thanks and took it. "How did you like Bert?"

"He's an awesome horse." He settled in, picked up a fork and dug into his food. He wasn't happy that his mom had been upset by Ryker's phone call, but being reminded that his brother faced mortal danger every day made his issues puny by comparison. "My saddle fits great, too."

"I'm sure Faith would have loaned you hers if necessary."

He hadn't thought of that, but she probably would have. "I love my saddle. I've always figured on taking it."

"I know. I'm glad you can."

"Me, too." His mom had made a financial sacrifice to buy him that hand-tooled beauty when he'd graduated from high school. She'd encouraged him to make this journey ever since he'd started talking about it and the saddle had been a tangible way to show that she believed in him. He needed to keep that in mind.

"What about Faith's dad? Is he coming to dinner tomorrow night?"

"He is."

"Good. Deidre called to ask if Jim had accepted the invite."

Cody stopped eating long enough to take a sip of his beer. "Makes me wonder if she's interested in him."

"She might be, although maybe she just wants to find out how he likes the house she sold him. I hope that's all it is, because I don't think Jim's boyfriend material. Faith said he hasn't dated since her mom died. I can't picture a guy like that with a social butterfly like Deidre."

"You might be surprised." He repeated some of the conversation about Deidre.

"I'll bet he thinks she's a fireball because of her short red hair. If he'd met her when she was a brunette, he might not have said that."

"True, but there was something in his voice. I don't think he was talking about her hair, and I can see Deidre being intrigued with his *still waters run deep* vibe. He'd be a challenge for her and we all know she likes a challenge."

His mom smiled. "Cody, you're such a romantic."

"Got it from you." He knew he had a romantic streak, but he had a practical reason for hoping Jim and Deidre hit it off. If Jim found himself a lady friend, Faith might change her mind about the two-week limit she'd put on their relationship. She might consider spending more time with him after he came back from his trip.

"So it looks like we'll have a dinner party tomorrow night." His mom's expression grew animated. "I can wear my blinged-out jeans again."

"You only have one pair like that?"

"That's it. Mandy offered to make more, but that's a lot of trouble when I'll be done with them before you know it. Besides, she has a new project for her spare time."

"What's that?" He forked up the last bite of meatloaf.

"She's altering some clothes for Faith."

Cody nearly choked on his meatloaf, but he managed to cough it into his napkin. His mom got him some water and he made a production of drinking it and catching his breath. Mandy was altering Faith's clothes? WTF?

But he had to play it cool. "Sorry about that. I'm eating way too fast. I was starving. Great meal, Mom. What were you saying? I forgot."

She eyed him strangely, but then she shrugged, as if she'd accepted his excuse for choking. "Mandy's thrilled that Faith wants to upgrade her wardrobe. This morning she took Faith's measurements, and surprise, surprise, the woman has a dynamite figure under her baggy clothes."

"Whatdya know?" Cody guzzled half his beer in a series of swallows.

"I'm not sure what motivated her to make a change, but Mandy's all over it. If she gets the clothes tomorrow morning, I'll bet she'll spend the day sewing so Faith can have something fun and flirty to wear tomorrow night."

"Sounds great." This dinner party was turning into a nightmare.

He'd have to make pleasant conversation with Jim Underwood, despite the fact that he was secretly getting horizontal with the man's daughter whenever possible. And that was only for starters. Even though he and Faith had enjoyed two passionate and very naked episodes, he was supposed to treat her like a casual acquaintance. Now it seemed she'd appear wearing a sexy outfit and he couldn't react to that, either. He wasn't the guy for this assignment. Sure as shootin', he'd blow their cover.

"Dessert?"

He glanced at his mom and back to his plate. He'd managed to eat every speck of food while he'd been cogitating this turn of events. It was a wonder he hadn't licked the plate while engrossed in his thoughts of the lovely and puzzling Faith Underwood. Why had she chosen this particular time to ditch the baggy clothes?

Pressing his hand to his stomach, he shook his head. "Thanks, but I'm stuffed." Stuffed with questions and no answers. Worse yet, he'd made a mistake in conducting this affair. He'd never snagged Faith's cell number.

He must have figured he wouldn't need it because he'd see her every day. But he wanted to see her *now* and find out what was going on with this wardrobe switcheroo. She hadn't mentioned it during their time together this evening, so she must be planning to surprise him.

He briefly considered driving over late tonight and tossing pebbles at her window. But what would he say that wouldn't sound stupid and chauvinistic? *I don't want you showing your body off to anyone but me?* Yeah, no. He wouldn't be saying that even if he was thinking it.

He'd say nothing, do nothing, and see how this all played out. He was mystified, though. She didn't need to alter her appearance for him. She already had him in the palm of her hand.

Pushing back his plate, he glanced at his mom. "Why don't you go relax and read your book? I'll take care of the cleanup."

"That would be terrific."

She paused on her way out of the kitchen. "I have a favor to ask for tomorrow."

"Name it."

"Jim's never seen the house. I'd like to have Faith help me with some cleaning and food prep. Would you be willing to handle her job at the stables?"

"You bet."

"Zane'll be there early, too. It'll give you boys a chance to talk."

"Good idea. It's weird having him living over at Mandy's house."

"His house, too, now."

"I know, but it was Mandy's and Aunt Jo's for so long. I'm still getting used to the change. Zane was always here."

"If it makes you feel any better, it feels strange to me, too. Having you around, even for a couple of weeks, helps."

What a concept. His mom had been surrounded by people until the day she wasn't. "Do you get lonely?"

She faced him, her blue eyes open and honest. "Sometimes. But my dearest wish is that all of you find a life that makes you happy. If that's nearby, I'll enjoy seeing you more often. If it's far away, I'll treasure the times you visit. It's not up to you boys to keep me company."

"Thanks, Mom. But the thing is, I enjoy your company." As he hugged her, his heart swelled with love.

Giving him a tender smile, she left the kitchen. He'd missed seeing that smile on a regular basis. Although he'd always assumed he'd go back to the Triangle V after finishing his trip, that prospect was losing its appeal. Maybe it was time to come home.

13

Faith had arranged to drop her bundle of clothes off at Zane and Mandy's house on her way to work.

Mandy acted as if Faith had given her a priceless artifact. "I've had the most fantastic idea! I've already emailed my boss in New York and she loves it. She thinks the timing's perfect. And it's all because of you!"

Faith stood in the entryway trying to make sense of what Mandy was saying. "I don't get it."

"Upcycle fashion! We'll call it *Americana*!" Mandy was still dressed in her fleece bathrobe and slippers. When she waved her arms around, the sleeves flapped dramatically. "Out here I have access to dozens of used clothing stores that are chock full of jeans and Western shirts."

"That's certainly true."

"We'll source from those stores. What I'm about to do with your outfits can be done to all of them. I'll take pictures of your altered clothes before I return everything to you, to give the designers in New York some ideas. But I know them. They'll take the concept and run with it."

Faith blinked. "That's brilliant. I hope you'll get famous for that idea."

"I don't know if I'll get famous. But I've already been promised a big fat bonus if this goes the way they expect. I'll use it to help with the raptor program. Zane's always wanted to buy his own medical equipment."

"I didn't know that."

"He's been making do because his buddy Kyle's been using his, but that's awkward. Either Kyle has to transport stuff over here or Zane has to take the injured bird to Kyle's office. The new building will be finished in another couple of months and I'd love to see Zane get that equipment this summer."

"Mandy, that would be wonderful." She gave her friend a hug. "Fingers crossed you get your bonus."

"I think I will, but first things first. Sometime around four this afternoon, I will bring you something amazing to wear for the dinner tonight. That was the goal, to upgrade your wardrobe, and that's going to happen before all the rest."

"I appreciate that, but it sounds as if this idea is a lot bigger than improving my wardrobe. If you need to spend the day working remote with your people in New York, I can wait." She'd rather not wait too long, though. She wanted Cody to get an eyeful of the new look.

"You most certainly will not! I intend to finish at least one outfit and then let everyone admire you. I guarantee I'll get as much of a thrill out of that as you will. I'll be over around four."

"I'll watch for you." Giving Mandy another hug, Faith left and drove to Wild Creek Ranch. Following her usual routine, she went straight to the barn to help feed. She found Cody and Zane distributing hay flakes from the wheelbarrow sitting in the aisle.

The sight of Cody, his muscles flexing as he manhandled the flakes of hay, warmed every cell in her body. "I'm sorry if I'm late. I can take over, now, if you have things to do."

"You're not late." He met her gaze and his blue eyes heated. "Hello, Faith."

The way he said it stirred her blood. There was something different about his attitude, though, and she couldn't decide what it was. "Hello, Cody. You're relieved."

"Mom asked me to fill in for you because she wants some help cleaning house and fixing tonight's dinner."

"Oh! Well, thank you, then. I should get up there."

"She'll be glad to see you."

She lowered her voice so Zane couldn't hear. "Are you?"

"I'm always glad to see you."

"Same here." She couldn't get a handle on his mood. "Talk with you later."

"Maybe not. I'll be gone most of the day looking at trailers. Zane's given me a bunch of new leads."

"Good luck with that." She hoped his mention of a trailer search wasn't some sort of signal. The subject of trailers had become loaded with significance now that she knew the purchase of one was the only thing keeping him here. "I'll see you tonight then, at dinner."

"Yes, ma'am. Looking forward to it."

Something was up with that cowboy. She tried to guess what that could be as she walked to the ranch house. He'd told her he was terrible at disguising his feelings and that was true because he wasn't acting the way he had the evening before.

But what had changed in the time they'd been apart? She wished they'd figured out a new rendezvous spot and set up a time to meet. Other than tonight's dinner, they wouldn't be seeing each other except during working hours.

This dinner party had thrown a monkey wrench into their plans, but she couldn't very well be upset about it. This morning before she'd left the house her father mentioned how much he was looking forward to going.

When she walked into the ranch house, Kendra was in house-cleaning mode. She'd put her dark hair into a ponytail and eighties music blasted from her bookshelf speakers. With a dust rag in one hand and a bottle of lemon polish in the other, she dusted the bookshelf while her hips moved with the beat. She couldn't dance yet, but she could wiggle.

She glanced over at Faith and raised her voice to be heard over the music. "Hi! I'll dust and you can vacuum!"

"Sure thing!" She was encouraged by how much Kendra could do by herself these days. Even better, her recovery wouldn't mean the end of Faith's employment. Kendra had promised to keep her on and finance the extra employee cost by taking on more riding students.

Deidre was the first additional one to come along. As Faith used the hose attachment to vacuum the furniture, her dad's unexpected comments yesterday percolated. There had been something in his voice, something new.

Maybe reading the books under her bed was making her see romance around every corner. But she couldn't shake the idea that her dad liked Deidre for more than her real estate expertise. That was unsettling.

She liked Deidre, too, but she'd never expected her dad to have a girlfriend. When she was around eight, she'd asked him if she'd ever have a stepmother. He'd told her that he'd married his soul mate and he figured a person only got one of those in a lifetime.

That conversation had been pivotal. She'd asked. He'd answered. Case closed. But what if he'd changed his mind? He and Deidre didn't seem like they matched, though. He was quiet and reserved, while Deidre—well, he'd said it himself. She was a fireball.

She'd been concentrating so hard on the subject that she'd finished her task without realizing it. She switched the vacuum off. Kendra was still dusting. And singing along with the music. Faith smiled. This dinner might be a pain in the neck for her, but Kendra was into it.

She waited until Kendra had finished the song. "Vacuuming's done. What next?"

"Coffee break." Kendra flipped the rag over an end table and lifted her arms in triumph. "If I dared, I'd do a Rocky dance. That's the first time I've dusted the entire living room." She grinned at Faith.

"Congratulations."

She gave a little bow. "Thank you. But I need to sit down." She sank into one of the easy chairs.

"Then let me make the coffee." Faith headed for the kitchen and started it brewing.

"There's a little bit of cake left over from Cody's welcome home dinner," Kendra called after her. "We should finish it up. Deidre's bringing two pies tonight, apple and cherry, so I need room in the fridge for leftovers."

"Cake sounds terrific, thanks!" Her dad would be happy about the pies. He liked pie better than cake and those two kinds were his favorites.

She dished the cake and took it in while the coffee finished. "This looks yummy."

"Jo is the best all-around cook I know and her chocolate cake is to die for. But we all agree that Deidre is a genius with pie crusts. I just buy the frozen kind but she makes them from scratch. Wait until you taste one of her pies. Amazing."

"Making good crusts is a skill. I just buy the frozen kind, too." She went to fetch the coffee.

When she came back with two steaming mugs, Kendra thanked her for waiting on her. "I hope in another month or so I can wait on you for a change."

Faith sat down in the other easy chair and gave her a smile. "That doesn't seem right. You being the boss, and all."

"As you might have noticed, we're not particularly formal around here regarding the boss/employee relationship. You feel more like family to me."

"That's nice to hear." She'd debated long and hard as to whether having an affair with Cody was a violation of Kendra's trust. Eventually she'd decided it wasn't because the relationship was short term. It wouldn't affect work at the ranch in any way because there would be no drama involved. Cody was an adult and he'd chosen to be involved with her on a limited basis.

Kendra would never have to know unless Cody told her about it, but he'd promised not to. Still, as Faith sat having coffee and cake with the person who was technically her boss, she felt a twinge of guilt. She would have preferred to be completely honest with Kendra on all matters. But this was too personal and she wasn't sure how Kendra would react. She might not like it.

Kendra balanced her cake plate on her lap and reached for her coffee mug. "Cody said Bert was a dream to ride."

"He's a fine horse."

"And you're a generous person to loan him out for this adventure of Cody's."

"It should be a good thing for Bert to get ridden that much. He needs the exercise." But there was that twinge of guilt again. Bert had come with strings attached.

"I'm excited for Cody that he's finally making his dream a reality."

"Me, too."

"I don't know how many fifteen-year-olds would have set that kind of goal, saved the money, and been ready to follow through almost ten years later."

"Not many."

"I know I sound like a proud mama, so you'll have to forgive me, but I admire that kind of dedication. He's voluntarily taking two months out of his life to concentrate on natural beauty. If everybody did that, we'd probably all be happier."

"Probably so." Faith met her gaze and smiled. "You have every right to be proud of him."

Kendra laughed. "And you're being very patient while I brag about my son. But mainly I want to thank you for loaning him Bert. That's a generous thing to do and makes it easier for him to go. If I know Cody, he'll come up with some creative way to thank you."

"Whoops, I think I forgot to shut off the coffee pot." She dashed for the kitchen and prayed Kendra hadn't noticed she was blushing.

"No worries! It'll shut off automatically."

"You're right." She took a deep breath and returned to the living room. "It's an old habit. When I lived in the bunkhouse they had a pot that didn't turn off by itself. It started a fire, which made a huge impression on me."

"Nothing wrong with being overly cautious with coffee pots." Kendra seemed to accept Faith's behavior as perfectly natural.

But it had been a close call. Faith was more than ready to stop discussing Cody. She asked what the next chore was and within a few minutes they'd finished their coffee and were back to cleaning. They worked well together and by noon the house was sparkling. Even the windows had been washed inside and out.

They spent the first half of the afternoon prepping the food for dinner. Kendra glanced at the clock when they were finished. "It sure goes fast when two of us are working on it. I have an idea, since we have time. Let's create some bouquets. I'll sit on the porch with the vases and arrange whatever wildflowers you bring me."

"That'll be fun."

"This time of year I love having wildflowers in the house, but I'm not up to gathering them. Mandy would help but I keep forgetting to ask her."

"I'd be happy to be your official wildflower gatherer this summer." Faith was so new to home ownership that she hadn't considered such a thing, but now she would.

"The vases are in the top of the cupboard over the stove. I usually fill them with water before I take them out there. Wildflowers wilt so fast you want to get them in water as soon as possible."

Faith climbed on a stepstool and opened the cupboard. "So pretty!"

"I actually have too many. My sweet boys have given me several arrangements from Perfect Petals over the years and I've kept the vases. Do you need some?"

"Oh, no, I couldn't take one of your precious vases."

"Of course you can. I'll never use them all. Look, there are two light blue ones that are almost identical. Take one of those."

"All right, I will." She lifted one down and put it on the counter. "Dad will probably love having some flowers in the house. I just never thought of it."

"Ian used to gather them for me."

Faith turned and caught the wistful expression on Kendra's face. "Doesn't this make you sad, then?"

"No, because he would have wanted me to keep gathering wildflowers."

"I'm sure you're right." Obviously Kendra was strong but that statement gave Faith a glimpse of how that strength had manifested itself. "How many vases should I get down?"

"Let's do five. That'll keep us busy for a while."

Faith glanced at the kitchen clock. Past three. Mandy could show up anytime with the altered outfit. Gathering wildflowers would be a good way to pass the time so she wouldn't get too impatient.

She transferred the vases filled with water to the front porch, took gloves and gardening shears that Kendra had in the pantry, and went in search of flowers. She found a lot of them up on the hill near the aviary where Zane was still keeping his raptors until the new facility was completed. She moved quietly so she wouldn't startle the injured birds.

She'd never learned the names of wildflowers, but these would make a colorful bouquet of purple, yellow and white. She brought them back to Kendra.

"Beautiful! There's usually a big patch on the far side of the house." Kendra began arranging the flowers in a vase.

Faith discovered a bonanza there. She made two trips to the porch. She was on her way to gather more when she heard Kendra yell. Dropping the shears, she took off running. If Kendra had fallen and hurt her leg...but no, she was standing on the porch holding a vase in one hand. She'd propped the door open with another.

She turned to Faith. "Damn it, I can't believe this!"

"What happened?" Faith bounded up the steps.

"I propped the door open so I could carry in a bouquet and a stupid squirrel ran right past me into the house!"

"Shitfire."

"My thoughts, exactly."

"We have to get it out of there." She looked at Kendra. "Any ideas?"

"I'm not squirrel savvy. And I'm slower than an arthritic turtle so I won't be much help."

"Look, the last thing we need is you falling. Stay right here and watch to see if it runs out. I'll...I'll creep in and try to locate it."

"Then what?"

"Then...I don't know. Are you sure it was a squirrel?"

"Yes!" Kendra waved her arm in the air.

"Shh. You'll scare it."

Kendra lowered her voice and leaned closer. "It's already scared, and yes, it's a squirrel. What else could it be?"

"Something tamer. A kitten."

"We don't have any kittens around here, Faith."

"I know. I was just hoping that maybe—"

"Trust me, it was a squirrel."

Faith peered in the door. "How big?"

"You know. Squirrel sized. Are you afraid of squirrels?"

"Not when they're in the wild."

"This one's in the house."

"I'm aware of that. And I'm not afraid of them, exactly, but it's just that...they move so fast. And they don't like being cornered. They could leap out and...bite in self-defense."

"Yeah, I'm afraid of them, too."

"All right." Faith took a deep breath. "I'm going in."

14

Cody stayed away from the ranch until he couldn't stand it anymore. He was sick of looking at trailers he had no intention of buying, at least not today. If they were still available next week, then fine. He'd also been haunted by the way he'd spoken to Faith that morning.

He'd been a total jerk and he had no excuse. If Faith wanted Mandy to streamline her clothes so she looked better, she had every right to do that. It might have nothing to do with him or everything to do with him, but they were her clothes, her body, her choice. He wanted to apologize. Then he wanted to find a quiet moment alone so they could figure out where to meet in private. For private deeds.

With any luck, she'd have finished helping his mom and would be down at the barn. But when he drove in...uh-oh. Something strange was going on. His mom stood on the porch near the open door with vases of wildflowers by her feet. He parked and got out of the truck. The noise level indicated a fight going on inside—furniture toppling, glass breaking and...Faith yelling?

He sprinted toward the porch, determined to rescue her from...from whatever was making her yell like that.

His mom put out her arm like a traffic cop, blocking his way. "Don't go in there."

"But she needs me!"

"I asked if she wanted help and she said this is a one-woman job."

"What's she doing?"

"Chasing a squirrel."

"A squirrel?" As something heavy fell to the floor with a thud, he took hold of his mother to move her out of the way.

She turned and gave him The Look that promised dire consequences if he defied her. "I mean it, Cody. Stay out. She said another person would make it worse. She had the cojones to go in there after it, and we will respect her wishes. Understood?"

His exhaled. "But—"

"Understood?"

"Yes, ma'am." He cringed as a bunch of things hit the floor in rapid succession. He'd guess books were falling off the shelf.

"Oh, no, you don't!" Faith got louder, followed by the sound of a broom hitting something soft, probably the upholstery, but maybe the squirrel. "Other way, you damned rodent! *Other way*!"

He wouldn't want to be that varmint right now. Faith was on the warpath, something he'd never seen before. Kind of fascinating.

"He's coming out!" She shouted the warning a split second before a gray streak whizzed past them and sailed down the steps, airborne. At the bottom, the squirrel got his legs under him and took off like his bushy tail was on fire.

Faith came to the door wearing a triumphant smile. Her braid was coming undone, her cheeks were flushed and she'd managed to rip the shoulder seam of her plaid shirt. Her chest heaved as she propped the broom handle on the floor like a victory flag. "The living room's a mess, but the squirrel's gone. And unharmed." Her gaze flicked toward Cody before returning to Kendra.

Kendra hobbled forward and gave her a hug. "Thank you. My fault, totally my fault."

"Nah." Faith hugged her back. "You couldn't know a squirrel was lying in wait hoping you'd leave the door open. But we have some work ahead of us to get things back to normal."

"I'm here to help." Cody wished he could hug Faith, too. But in this scenario, he didn't have that privilege. He might be able to pass it off as a friendly gesture, but he didn't want to take the chance that he'd add a quick back rub to the hug.

Faith led the way into the living room, where the furniture had all been dragged out of position. The vase of wildflowers his mom must have brought in before this disaster started had been knocked to the floor, scattering broken glass, water and flowers.

The bookcase, which now blocked the hallway to the bedrooms, must have been hauled there by Faith. That could explain why the books had tumbled to the floor. Cody hurried to pick them up before water seeped in that direction. A lamp on an end table was in pieces on the floor, too.

But Faith had managed to close the door into the kitchen before the squirrel had made it in there. Dining room chairs had been knocked over, but the damage had been confined to the living room. Nothing other than the lamp and the vase had been broken.

"I'm sorry about the lamp, Kendra." Faith hurried over to help Cody pick up the books. "You have more vases, but you probably won't find a match for that lamp."

"Matching lamps are so last century, don't you think?" Kendra surveyed the room. "It's not so bad."

Faith stood, a pile of books in her arms. "Compared to what? The Titanic?"

"You don't know what a disaster zone is until you've raised five boys who love to wrestle in the living room."

Cody objected. "We only broke one thing, and you finally admitted you hated that horse statue."

"I did hate it. The horse had a mean look on its face. But the couple who gave it to me boarded four horses with us so I had to display it. Ugly damn thing."

Cody went over and wrapped an arm around her shoulders. "Then I'll confess. I'm the one who broke it."

His mom laughed. "Nice try. It was a joint effort. You'd better go fetch the mop and bring a dustpan while you're at it. The broom's already in here, which must have been a neat trick. Faith, how did you get the broom without letting the squirrel in the kitchen?"

"I'm not sure. It all happened so fast."

Cody gazed at her in admiration. "You're amazing." She was stronger than he'd thought if she could drag a loaded bookcase across the opening into the hallway.

"You would have done the same."

He grinned. "Not me. I'm scared of squirrels." He wasn't, but he'd said it so she'd give him a smile. Which she did. His little joke didn't make up for his crappy behavior earlier today, but it was a start.

The three of them had nearly finished cleaning up the mess when Mandy walked through the door, a Neiman-Marcus shopping bag in one hand. "Hey, is this the cleaning detail for tonight's party?"

"I accidentally let a squirrel in the house," Kendra said. "Faith saved the day, but there was a slight kerfuffle before the squirrel was sent packing."

"Actually it was an epic struggle." Cody stood. "Faith was a superhero, woman versus rodent, and she came out ahead." He knew the altered clothes would be in that Neiman-Marcus bag and he'd be enthusiastic no matter what.

"I don't doubt that Faith stepped up." Mandy held out the bag in her hand. "For you, victorious lady."

In contrast with her assertive behavior with the squirrel, Faith seemed shy about the new outfit.

She got up from the floor where she'd been wiping the last of the water and accepted the bag. "Thanks, Mandy. I hope you didn't spend your entire day on this."

"I'm not saying if I did or I didn't, but I had fun, and that's been a rarity for me in my work recently. I'm excited about this concept. I'd ask you to model the outfit now, but…you'd probably rather not."

"I'm really grubby right now. I'd like to get cleaned up first." She didn't look at Cody.

His heart turned over. She wanted to make a good impression on him. He was sure of it, now. Even though their relationship was temporary, she wanted him to see her in clothes that flattered her. She wanted him to think she looked nice. Sexy.

Now he was thoroughly ashamed of himself for being touchy about it. He needed to talk with her but wasn't sure how he could manage it with his mom and Mandy around.

"Speaking of getting cleaned up," his mother said. "Faith and I could both use some time to do that after the squirrel incident. Cody, you look fresh as a daisy. Would you finish here while Faith goes home to change and I slip into my fancy pants? Zane will be over soon to feed and if you could help him, that would be wonderful, too."

"Absolutely."

"I'll walk Faith to her truck," Mandy said. "I want to explain the alterations I did."

That meant Cody was neatly locked out of any chance to speak with Faith before dinner tonight. But he'd done it to himself. They could have had a quick conversation this morning but he'd blown that chance. His loss.

He'd make an opportunity tonight, somehow. She'd be here with her dad, which would complicate things, but he'd invent some excuse. He couldn't let her drive away after dinner without knowing they had a plan. He needed her.

* * *

Two hours later, Cody hadn't managed to shower but he'd at least shaved and changed his shirt. Then he went into the kitchen to help his mom finish up dinner preparations. She had on the jeans Mandy had created for her and she'd added a sparkly top, an upswept hairdo, and fancy earrings.

He pulled the pork chop and scalloped potato main dish out of the oven while she put together a salad. "You look great tonight, Mom." He set the heavy dish on the tile counter and covered it with foil.

"Thanks. I feel great. Breaking my leg taught me how lucky I've been regarding my health. This is the first major issue I've had, which is more than a lot of people can say. I'll appreciate it so much more when I can walk and dance and ride the way I used to."

"You'll get there.""

"Can't wait." She picked up the bottle of dressing and shook it hard before dribbling it over the salad. "By the way, your gut instincts about Deidre and Jim might be right. She's bringing both a cherry *and* an apple pie."

"Damn, that's good news. But don't take it as a sign that she's after Jim. I can tell you exactly who she's bringing those pies for."

"Who?"

"Me."

His mom was still laughing about that when the doorbell rang. "Hey, the doorbell!" She looked startled. "I just realized nobody uses it! Who could that be?"

"My money's on Faith and her dad. She might not come in if she has him with her."

"You're probably right."

"I'll get it." He prepared himself to see Faith looking different, but he didn't prepare well enough. When he opened the door, he almost didn't recognize her.

She wore makeup, for one thing. It looked nice on her, but he wasn't used to it. Her eyes seemed bigger and her lips fuller. He could barely see her freckles, though, and he missed those.

Her hair was down, but it wasn't straight anymore. Instead it fell in gentle waves to her shoulders. Because her green plaid shirt fit her, he could see exactly where her shoulders were. And her breasts, which strained the material just enough to make his groin tighten.

Green, gem-like buttons had replaced the original ones and they started lower, which gave him a glimpse of cleavage. She'd tucked the form-fitting shirt into jeans that showcased her hour-glass figure instead of hiding it. Her belt was studded with sparkly green gems that matched the buttons on her shirt. Even her boots looked different.

He swallowed. "Wow."

That must have been the right reaction, because her expression changed from uncertain to happy. "Can we come in?"

"Oh! Sure!" He stepped back from the open door. "Sorry, I just—"

"I know, son." Jim patted his shoulder as he walked by. "Gave me quite a start, too."

His mom came hobbling out of the kitchen and went wild over Faith's new look while somehow managing to introduce herself to Faith's dad at the same time. Cody noticed the green bling on the back pockets of Faith's jeans two seconds before his mom made her turn around so she could examine her from all sides.

While she was busy exclaiming over the sparkles and the cascade of red-gold curls, Faith glanced at him and smiled. "You might want to close that door, Cody. I'd hate to have a squirrel get in."

"Uh, right." Damn, his face got hot as he turned around and shut the door.

The last time he'd felt this dazed and confused was when he'd accidentally beaned himself on a tree branch while out riding with his brothers. Faith was so...he didn't even have the words for it, but he sensed that her transformation was a game changer.

Unconsciously he'd relished the teacher-pupil dynamic in this relationship. When she was the one asking and he was the one graciously giving, the balance of power had been in his favor. But he could say goodbye to that bullshit. The power had just shifted.

* * *

Cody's initial reaction had been everything Faith had hoped for. She wished they were free to exchange hot glances across the table, but that would arouse suspicion. During dinner, she'd caught him looking at her, though, and he was clearly thinking about something. She hoped it was their next rendezvous.

Meanwhile Mandy was telling everyone about her new idea. Faith had Mandy to thank for the curls and the makeup. She'd asked Faith to stop by on the way to the ranch, and while Zane had taken Faith's dad over to see the progress on the new raptor headquarters, Mandy had worked her magic. Then she'd snapped a bunch of pictures to send to New York.

She'd mentioned during dinner that Faith and her dad had stopped by for a quick photo shoot, but she hadn't said anything about the hair and makeup session. Faith was glad about that. Cody had been so awestruck by her new look that she didn't want to destroy the illusion by discussing her makeover.

Talk of Faith's outfit and Mandy's plans for a line of recycled clothing dominated the conversation for a good part of the meal. Kendra and Deidre were enthusiastic, and naturally Mandy's mom, Jo, was, too. Zane and Cody chimed in with a few comments. Only Faith's dad remained silent. Faith wanted to draw him into the conversation, but fashion wasn't his thing and besides, he didn't know this crowd and might be reluctant to offer an opinion.

Then Deidre turned to him. "Jim, you've been sort of quiet tonight. What do you think of Mandy's idea?"

Faith expected her dad to say it was fine and leave it at that.

"Oh, it'll go gangbusters." He leaned toward Mandy. "And I think it's great that you're going to use any extra income for the raptor project."

"It's dear to my heart."

"I can see why. I had no idea that was going on. The headquarters will be something. I've always been a fan of those amazing birds."

Faith blinked. On the drive from Zane and Mandy's house to the ranch, her dad had expressed admiration for Zane and Mandy's dedication to the raptors but the trip had been short and they'd had little time to discuss it. She'd had no idea he was so enthusiastic.

Then he looked over at Deidre. "Zane also told me about the contribution you and your posse have been making to the cause. What's the name you gave yourselves?"

"The Whine and Cheese Club. But it's not my posse. All five of us are in charge." She glanced at Jo and Kendra. "Right?"

"Damn straight," Kendra said with a grin.

"Well, I'd like to meet the other two and shake their hands. You're all doing good work." He turned to Faith. "Do you know about these ladies, honey bun?"

"A little bit." Kendra's high school girlfriends fascinated her. She'd never had a best friend in school, let alone three of them. They weren't stuck up about it, either. They'd invited Jo to be the fifth member of their club even though she hadn't gone to school with them.

"All I can say is, I'm impressed." He gazed at Deidre. "Mighty impressed." He took a sip of his beer.

Faith's world tilted. She'd never seen her dad look at a woman the way he was looking at Deidre. She'd never seen a woman looking back at her dad the way Deidre was doing, either. She needed to talk to Cody. Now.

Acting on impulse, she faked a headache. She'd never done it but she'd read about it in her books. "I hate to admit this, Dad, but I feel a headache coming on."

Her dad turned to her immediately. "Honey bun, I'm so sorry. We'll go."

"No, Dad, you stay. Cody can run me home."

"Absolutely." Cody pushed back his chair. "Jim, stay and have some of Deidre's pie. I promise you it's excellent. You'll want to try both kinds. I've got this."

Her dad looked torn. "I confess I was looking forward to a slice of that pie."

"Then it's settled. I'll catch a ride with Cody. You stay and enjoy your pie."

"I'll get my keys." Cody left the dining room.

While he was gone, Faith thanked Kendra for a wonderful dinner. Everyone told her to feel better and she had to assure Kendra a couple of times that the squirrel incident hadn't caused her headache. Then she went out the front door with Cody.

He didn't say anything until they'd left the porch. "Do you really have a headache?"

"No."

"Thank God. I was hoping you were okay." He squeezed her hand as he helped her into the truck. "I'd kiss you now but I don't dare. I'll wait until it's safer."

The minute he got in the truck, she turned to him. "Did you see how they looked at each other?"

"Your dad and Deidre?"

"Who else? What do you think it means?"

"I'm not qualified to answer that." He backed around and started down the dirt road at a faster than usual speed.

"I think they're into each other."

"Maybe. Is that a problem?"

"Yes. No. Oh, I don't know! But it feels weird, like I suddenly looked up and the sky was green instead of blue. He's never been interested in a woman before. And Deidre's so different from him." She held onto the armrest as the truck jolted down the road. "What if she's not right for him?"

"Then I suppose they'll figure that out."

Not the reassurance she was looking for. "And why her?" The truck hit another bump. "What's the attraction?"

"I'm only guessing, but he seems to be drawn to her dynamic personality. And she's drawn to...I'm not sure what."

"Hey! He's a wonderful guy!"

"I know. I didn't mean it that way, but you're right that they're very different. Maybe she's looking for serenity. Your dad's very serene."

"He won't be serene for long if he hooks up with Deidre." The ride smoothed out when they reached the paved road.

"That could be the idea. He's tired of being serene all the time. He wants some excitement in his life."

"I suppose it's possible." She let her head flop back. ""He really came alive just now. And I want him to be happy, but he hasn't looked twice at anyone since my mom died and that's been twenty-four years. Why is he changing now?"

"Because you are."

She glanced at him in surprise. "I am not! Well, maybe on the outside some, but I'm the same person inside. And besides, he made that fireball remark before I put on these clothes. My new look can't be the reason he's showing interest in Deidre."

"Have you ever invited a guy to go out riding with you before?"

"No, but he has no idea what we've been up to. As far as he's concerned, you were taking Bert for a test run."

"Which is another thing. You're loaning me your beloved horse. Your dad recognizes that you must think well of me. He may not have figured out we're having sex, but he's noticed that you like me. A lot."

"You don't think he believes I'm doing it out of gratitude to the McGavins?"

"Nope."

She sighed. "That's bad news. If you're right, then I helped create this situation."

"And what if it's a good situation?"

"That remains to be seen. He could end up getting hurt."

"Guess so." He was silent for a bit. "I think I know, but I still have to ask. What prompted you to have Mandy alter your clothes?"

"You did. You make me feel desirable. I want to look sexy for you all the time and not just when I'm naked."

"You looked sexy to me in your old clothes."

"Come on, not really. Not until you'd seen me naked. Then you could picture what was underneath. You said you liked being the only person besides me who knew that secret."

His chest heaved. "I did say that, and it was a selfish comment. There's no reason you should dress in baggy clothes so that I have exclusive info about your great body. I apologize for that and for acting like a jackass this morning in the barn."

"You were acting weird. Why?"

"Mom told me last night that you'd asked Mandy to alter some of your clothes. I was surprised. And a little upset."

"Why were you upset?"

"I'd rather not tell you."

"But if you don't tell me, I might imagine something worse."

He didn't answer right away. Then he took a deep breath. "It's like you and I are in this secret club and nobody else knows what's going on. But by changing your outfits, you've given them a clue. And you didn't tell me about it first. In fact, I was the last to know."

She'd hurt his feelings. But he was a guy, so she probably shouldn't point that out. "I wanted to do something special to surprise you."

"I know that, now."

"I hoped that you'd see me in these clothes and be consumed by lust."

"As it happens, I am." He shifted in his seat.

"Then my outfit is turning you on?"

"Yes."

"By the way, where are we?"

"On a lonely road where nobody goes except lovers who want to have sex."

"How do you know this? Wait, don't tell me."

"I wasn't going to." He pulled off on a dirt path and drove into the trees.

Her body warmed with anticipation, but she was concerned about not being home when her dad got there. "Do we have time for this?"

"You betcha. We're not that far from your house, believe it or not. I've sat around the ranch house dinner table enough to know that we have at least thirty minutes before I need to run you home. Since you supposedly have a headache, you can make a beeline for your room and stay there. You don't have to show your face when your dad comes back."

"Why wouldn't I show my face?"

"Because right now you look like a fashion model. After I finish making love to you, your lipstick will be gone, your mascara will be smeared, your shirt will be wrinkled and you'll be wearing a big ol' grin. He'd know exactly what you and I have been doing."

15

Cody had no sooner turned off the engine than Faith reached for the door handle. He laid a restraining hand on her arm. “Hang on. Let me get the back open, first.”

“I can help.”

“Let me do it and preserve my macho image.”

She laughed. “All right.”

Leaving his hat on the dash, he climbed down and started around to the back of the truck. He loved that she was so eager. Maybe that was only because she was new at this, but he cherished her enthusiasm.

Consequently, he wanted to keep this thing between them alive for longer than another week or so. Now he had some hope that he could. Faith had set something in motion without realizing all the unintended consequences.

She’d planned on changing just one thing, her virginal status, and keeping everything else the same. She hadn’t counted on a domino effect. Not surprising since this was the first time she’d taken a major step on her own.

The dominoes would probably fall whether she wanted them to or not. She might think she was falling, too. If that happened, he wanted to be there to catch her.

In the meantime, though, he would spend as much time with her as he could to strengthen the bond between them. Tonight's opportunity had fallen in his lap, but he'd put some solid plans in place before dropping her off at her house.

After opening the window and the tailgate, he crawled part way in and grabbed the lantern. Turning it on low, he tucked it along the side of the mattress. He wouldn't have candlelight this time but she likely wouldn't mind. And he didn't have to worry about cows licking his butt, either.

He wasn't gone long, but by the time he came back she'd taken off everything except her bra. Her clothes lay folded on the driver's seat and she was leaning forward to unhook her bra.

"Allow me." He nudged her hands aside and finished the job. "Trying to save time?" He drew her bra down over her arms. The dome light revealed her freckled breasts tipped with rosy nipples that had already begun to peak. His body grew taut. God, how he wanted her.

Smiling, she took the bra and added it to the pile. "Saving time and making sure nothing happens to my clothes."

"Aw, Faith." He turned her to face him. "Did I worry you by saying I'd wrinkle your shirt?" He crouched down and gazed into her eyes. "I'm sorry."

She didn't look worried. Instead she looked turned on. "Don't be sorry. I wanted you to be driven to a frenzy by my outfit. That was the idea."

"It worked." He combed her hair forward so it curled around her breasts. Crouching like this pinched his privates, but the view was outstanding.

"In the books, when a man sees a woman in a seductive outfit, sometimes he wants her so much he rips it off."

"I like to think I wouldn't have gone that far. Mandy put a lot of effort into your clothes and I can tell you like them."

"But you still felt like ripping them off?"

"Yes, ma'am. If you must know, dinner was a living hell. Every time I looked at you I wanted to drag you outside, rip off your clothes and take you right there in the front yard." Slight exaggeration, but close enough.

"Oh, good." Her voice was wispy, like she was short on air.

"You were probably wise to take them off so I wouldn't be tempted to do that." He slid his hands under her hips. "Hold onto me. I'll carry you to the back of the truck."

"Did you bring condoms?" She wound her arms around his neck.

"Two." He scooped her up and she wrapped her legs around his hips. That put her right smack against the bulge in his jeans, which was both heaven and hell. "I grabbed them when I fetched my keys. But I think we'll only have time for—"

"You said we had thirty minutes."

"I know. And I brought a spare just in case." He nudged the door shut with his knee and the dome light flicked off. "But I still think we're looking at one time if we do it right."

She nestled against his crotch, her breath coming faster. "How about once up against the truck right now and then we'll go in the back?"

"You're kidding." He stopped in his tracks.

"Not kidding." She wiggled her sweet little ass. "In the books they do it against the wall but we're fresh out of walls." She drew in a quick breath. "I thought of it right after you went back there, which was another good reason to take off my clothes."

"The truck is metal. It'll be cold."

"I don't care. Brace me against the door, Cody. It'll be amazing."

His cock surged against the restriction of his briefs and jeans. "I'll agree with you on that point." Heart pounding, he put one booted foot on the running board and balanced her on his knee while he fished one of the condoms out of his jeans and tucked it in his shirt pocket. "But it might not be so comfortable."

"I don't want comfort." She gulped. "I want wild and crazy."

"Then that's what you'll get." He could deny her nothing. Her curiosity and willingness to try anything captivated him far more than he was ready to admit. "But you'll have to help."

Her voice quivered with excitement. "Just tell me what to do."

"I'll hold you, but you'll need to unfasten my jeans and put the condom on."

"Oh, something new! What fun."

"Mm." It would be something new, all right. Doing this with someone who understood how to roll on a condom was one thing. But she likely would fumble around. And he'd have to keep from coming. Ideally he should have taught her the art of condom application before trying this maneuver. Too late.

He tried to maintain his cool while she fiddled with his belt and the button on his jeans but he didn't have much luck. He was gasping for breath by the time she pulled down the zipper and shoved his briefs past his rigid cock. Cool air hit his overheated crotch and he closed his eyes as the sensation jacked up his level of arousal several notches.

"Your shirt's in the way." She yanked his shirt open and snaps popped in rapid succession.

"FYI, you can rip my clothes anytime."

She took out the foil packet and removed the condom. "I just might." Then she paused as if studying how best to proceed.

"Start at the top and roll it down."

"Right. I've got the idea."

She didn't have the idea, not by a long shot, and he was a hot mess by the time she finally got the damn thing on.

"Done." After that breathless announcement, she wound her arms around his neck again. "We're ready."

He spoke through gritted teeth. "Some of us more than others."

"You'll feel better in a minute."

"Or less. Put your hands on my shoulders. Get a good grip."

"I will."

When she slid her hands under his shirt and took hold, he remembered this was the same woman who'd hauled a loaded bookcase halfway across a room. She might leave a mark. He liked the thought of that.

Lifting her, he shifted his feet so he'd be balanced when he lowered her onto...oh, yeah. He groaned as gravity did its work. Her body had learned his and she accepted his full length in one smooth glide. He felt the twitch of an impending orgasm and tamped it down.

"Cody, I love this."

Her husky words, saturated with passion, nearly tipped him over the edge. His fingers flexed against her perfectly rounded ass. "Move with me, Faith. Follow my lead." He guided her upward and she pushed down on his shoulders. "Good. That's good."

In seconds, they'd established a rhythm, and he worked it, thrusting upward as she bore down, rotating his hips to increase her pleasure, widening his stance so he could give her everything he had.

Moonlight filtering through the trees provided enough light to watch her breasts shimmy and her eyes glitter. He could feel her tighten around him and he was perilously close. "Wild enough?"

She gasped. "Yes, oh, yes...I'm almost..."

"I know. I feel you." He'd never been so tuned into a woman's responses as he was to Faith's. Instinctively he knew how to move. A shift of angle, a faster stroke, and she'd...ah, there it was.

When she started to cry out, he leaned forward and covered her mouth with his. Her lipstick had a sweet flavor, like cherries. Swallowing her cries, he lifted his head so she could get some air. But he captured her lips again as he thrust one more time and shuddered, propelled into his climax by the enthusiasm of hers. When Faith came, she let his cock know it. Joining the party was just a matter of letting go.

Surrendering to that feeling had never been so sweet as it was with Faith. No matter how this crazy episode turned out, he'd never regret being a part of it.

When they both stopped shaking, she gazed at him in the silvery light of the moon overhead. "I couldn't ask for someone better than you."

His chest felt tight. "I could say the same. You might think I'm some kind of dream or fantasy, but so are you."

She smiled. "Okay, maybe I am a little bit, after I emerged from my cocoon. But you took me on when I was still an ugly duckling. That was a risky thing. I still don't know why you did."

"You needed me."

Her expression softened. "I did."

"I'm not sure you do anymore, at least not in the same way."

Her gaze sharpened. "Cody McGavin, did you buy a trailer?"

"Couldn't find one I liked."

She sighed in relief. "You had me worried for a second. I thought you were about to tell me you were leaving."

"Not yet."

"I'm glad. Now we need to untangle ourselves. Time's running out."

He wasn't sure if she meant for tonight or in a general sense, but in either case she was right. He chose to focus on the immediate issue, whether they could make it through a second round.

Setting it up turned into a comedy routine. She was barefoot, so he carried her to the tailgate while they were still linked together. They started laughing, which didn't help at all.

"I'll bet you've never executed this maneuver before." She grinned as he settled her on the tailgate and carefully withdrew.

"And I'll bet you've never sat bare-assed on the tailgate of a truck."

"Nope." She kicked her legs back and forth. "Feels sort of kinky."

"I'll take your word for it." He used his bandanna to remove the condom. "Doesn't appeal to me at all. You can crawl on in there whenever you've a mind to. I'm gonna shuck my clothes out here."

"Okay." She swung her legs up and got to her hands and knees.

While he undressed, he happened to catch that moment. "Now there's a picture."

She glanced over at him. "One more thing we haven't done."

"You've read about that position, too?"

"Yes, but we're not doing it tonight."

"Good. I can only stand so much excitement."

She waved a hand toward his bad boy, which already stood at attention. "Tell that to your friend."

"Yeah, well, he wants you all the time, six ways to Sunday." He took out a condom before dumping his clothes on the tailgate. He quickly rolled it on. She didn't need to be in charge again tonight. Maybe another night they'd practice.

"All the time?" She sat on the blanket just inside the opening and gazed at him.

"Pretty much." He climbed onto the tailgate. "Scoot back. I'm coming in."

"You think about having sex with me even when I'm not there?"

He crawled toward her and leaned in for a soft kiss. Nibbling gently on her lips, he guided her down to the cushy surface. "I think about you a lot. Not just sex, either."

"But mostly sex?"

"I wouldn't say that." He moved over her, nudging her thighs apart as he continued to drop tender kisses on her mouth and cheeks. Sure enough, he'd smeared her lipstick.

She ran her hands down his back. "I think about you a lot, too."

"That's nice." As if his cock knew the way, he found her slick entrance and eased inside. Lifting his head, he used lantern light to watch her expression as he slid deeper. "You look happy."

"I am happy." She lifted her hips and cupped his ass, urging him closer. "Having you inside me feels wonderful."

He pushed in tight. "It feels wonderful to me, too." He stayed very still. This moment, when they were as close as two people could be, felt special. It was time for them to start treating it that way. "I have an idea."

Her gaze held his and her voice was like a caress. "What?"

"Let's stop calling it sex. We're not just having sex anymore. We're making love."

"We are?"

"Yes, ma'am."

"How can you tell?"

He smiled. "For me, it's easy. When I do this..." He began a slow, steady rhythm. "It isn't just my cock that feels good. My heart does, too."

Her breath caught. "So does mine. Maybe we are making love."

"You know the good thing about that?" He leaned down and feathered a kiss over her cherry-flavored lips.

"What?" Her breath came faster as he picked up the pace.

"There's no wash, rinse, repeat. It gets better every time." And he did his level best to show her. Judging from the way she clutched his ass and cried out his name when she climaxed, he might have succeeded.

16

Faith beat her dad home, thank God. With an ear cocked for the sound of a truck, she wrote him a quick note saying she'd gone to bed. Then she hurried upstairs and closed herself in her room.

One look in her mirror had her grinning like an idiot, just as Cody had predicted. Her lipstick was mostly gone and she had raccoon eyes from the mascara. Her shirt wasn't wrinkled but she'd buttoned it wrong and she'd forgotten to zip her jeans. Her hair was tangled and the scent of Cody's aftershave clung to her skin. She'd been well and truly ravished.

And made love to. She undressed slowly in the dark while reliving every moment she and Cody had shared on that lonely road. Tomorrow she'd shower, but for now she wanted his scent to lull her to sleep.

She understood what he'd been hinting at by insisting they were making love instead of merely having sex. He thought they were falling for each other. That made her smile. He was assuming she hadn't fallen for him the first time she'd laid eyes on him.

If she hadn't completely fallen in love that day two months ago, then everything she'd managed to find out about him since then had clinched the deal. She'd known the day they'd met that he was beautiful on the outside. Since then, everybody who knew him had confirmed that he was beautiful on the inside, too. Maybe slightly spoiled, but kind and generous to a fault.

They'd been right. He'd agreed to be her lover for her sake, not his. He'd gone out of his way to make the experience romantic even when he hadn't felt romantically inclined toward her. But he was, now.

Although she was honored and gratified that he'd started to care for her, it didn't change anything as far as she was concerned. A man like Cody had surely been in love several times before and would be again. She didn't kid herself that she would turn out to be the love of his life. But he was hers, and when they parted at the end of next week, she'd hold this special time in her heart forever. It would be enough.

Congratulating herself on having chosen the perfect man for this once-in-a-lifetime experience, she set her alarm, snuggled under the covers and closed her eyes.

The noise of the front door opening and closing brought her awake. She glanced at the digital time on her phone. Her dad was home an hour later than Cody had estimated the dinner party would wrap up. And he was whistling.

A wave of uneasiness rippled across her warm contentment. She hadn't heard him whistle since before the accident. She thought of Cody's belief that her behavior might have triggered a change in her dad. She had trouble accepting that idea.

But Cody's remarks echoed in her head. Was there any chance her dad wanted to date, maybe even remarry? She couldn't imagine it, not after all this time. They'd just moved into this cute little house. They were starting to settle in and establish routines, like sitting on the porch to watch the sunset. She'd get back to doing that once Cody was gone.

Her alarm woke her from a hot dream involving Cody. For one delicious moment, she imagined what it would be like to roll over and find him there in bed with her. Then she threw off the covers and headed for the shower. Today she'd have to put on her normal clothes and braid her hair.

That was fine. She wouldn't dare work in the outfits Mandy was fixing for her. Maybe she'd have to request some plainer jeans and shirts, without any bling. She also should start paying for the work. Mandy had offered to do the fancy stuff for free, but she couldn't dazzle her New York design company with plain old work clothes.

Last night had been a Cinderella experience but the person who'd stayed out past curfew had been her dad. Why? Maybe the group had decided to play cards after dessert. She'd do a little fishing during breakfast and try to find out.

As usual, her dad was dressed and had coffee brewing by the time she came downstairs. He was cooking bacon and eggs, too, although often they just had cereal and toast. He wasn't whistling this morning but he sure did look cheerful.

He gave her a big smile when she walked into the kitchen. "Hey, there, honey bun. Headache all gone?"

"It is, Dad. Thanks." She got down plates, silverware and mugs. Then she snagged a couple of napkins from the holder and carried everything to the kitchen table. "Did you have a good time last night?"

"I had a great time. That Deidre bakes the best pies I've ever eaten. She made me take some home. I'm having pie with breakfast. Want some?"

"No, thanks."

"Suit yourself, but you're missing a treat."

Faith poured coffee into both mugs and tried to come up with a way of asking why he'd come in so late. "Kendra sure seems to like having company. It's a wonder that she doesn't get tired out, though, lugging that cast around."

"Oh, she does. We all helped clean up after dessert so she wouldn't have to."

"Lots of cleanup, huh?"

"Not much, with everybody pitching in." He dished out their eggs and bacon, put the skillet in the sink and came to sit at the table. "In fact, we all left before Cody came back from running you home."

"Huh." Something wasn't adding up.

"Since it was still so early, Deidre asked if I'd like to drive over and see her place."

Faith had her mug halfway to her mouth and she put it back down. "You went over to her *house*?"

"Yep. It's nice, but you'd expect that with her being a real estate agent."

Faith stared at him.

"Is something wrong, honey bun?"

She swallowed. "It's just that I can't remember a single time you've done anything remotely like this."

He gazed at her, his gray eyes searching hers. "Ah. You don't like it."

"I...I didn't say that."

"No, but you look quite startled."

"Because it's not like you. I don't know if you remember, but you told me years ago that my mother was your soul mate and a person only got one of those in a lifetime."

"I remember saying that and I expect it's probably true. But that doesn't mean I wouldn't consider spending time with someone like Deidre."

Her stomach tightened. "That's a change from how you've been before."

"Honey bun, I'm not the only one acting different. I've minded my own business up to now, but I can't help noticing that you're rather fond of Cody McGavin."

Oh, God, she was blushing. "He's a friend."

"Slightly more than that, I think."

"He's leaving next week on his trip. After that he's going back to his job at the guest ranch. We're friends, but...he's leaving." She couldn't make herself tell her father a bald-faced lie and say *we're just friends.*

"Do you wish he would stay?"

"Good grief, no! This trip means everything to him."

"I thought that you might have put on the pretty clothes in hopes he might not leave."

"Absolutely not."

"Then what made you decide to fix yourself up like that? Speaking of change, that was a big one. You looked real nice, but I confess I'm curious."

"I just noticed how great Mandy looks compared to my baggy outfits and I wanted...I wanted..." She ran out of words because Cody had been the reason, although she hadn't been trying to keep him here. Never that.

"You wanted to look nice for Cody?"

"That would be pointless, wouldn't it? He's leaving." She stared at her dad. "Is that why you went to Deidre's house? You thought I might run off with Cody?"

"Not run off, exactly, but—"

"I promise that's the last thing I'd ever do. I want to stay here with you in our house." Panic made her heart race. "It's perfect for just the two of us."

"That's true. I like our house very much. But when I see you with Cody, I realize I can't expect you to stay in this house with me forever. You say nothing will come of your friendship with him, but maybe another nice young man will come along."

"No, he won't, Dad. I'm not interested in finding a nice young man. I love this house and living with you. Nothing will change that, ever."

"You can't know that."

"Yes, I can!" She was yelling at her father. Horrified, she clapped a hand over her mouth. Then she took a deep breath. "I'm sorry, Dad. I just...want everything to stay the same. And it will. I promise."

His gaze was gentle as he laid his hand over hers. "You have to go or you'll be late."

She glanced at the kitchen clock. He was right. "Tell you what. Let's sit on the porch tonight and watch the sunset. We can talk more, then."

"I thought you might be taking another ride with Cody."

"No." In fact, she'd originally planned to tell her dad she'd be late coming home so that she and Cody could meet up on a back road. He'd be returning from town after another futile search for a trailer. It wasn't a perfect scheme but it was what they'd decided on for today.

But how could she do that now? Her dad would suspect what was going on even if he didn't know the details. He viewed her behavior as a major shift in their lives and he was ready to shift with it. Cody had been right. Changes she'd made had prompted changes in her dad. She'd never intended that. She didn't want it. *Life was perfect as it was*.

"Just so you know, I'm fine with it if you want to go riding with him."

"I'd rather sit on the front porch with you." Sitting with him was more important than being with Cody. If she reestablished cherished routines with her dad, then everything could get back to normal.

He peered at her. "Are you sure, honey bun?"

"Yes, I'm sure. Sorry I didn't finish my breakfast." She left the table, hurried through the living room and grabbed her backpack from beside the front door. Her battered hat hung on the wall and she crammed that on her head. Time to straighten out the mess she'd made.

On the drive to the ranch, she tried to remember what Cody had said he'd be doing first thing this morning. Later he'd go into town and pretend to look at trailers, but he had no reason to leave at dawn to do that.

He might have said he'd be down at the barn helping Zane. She'd been so focused on their evening plan that she hadn't paid attention. Now she needed to know where to find him.

She shook with dread, but she had to do this. Cody had always been like the grand piano the pioneers were forced to leave beside the trail. She'd never expected to keep him, only to treasure him for the short time they had together.

She'd just hoped that time could last a little longer. Turned out that wasn't a good idea. If she wanted to preserve the life she knew and loved, she had to act now.

Her dad obviously thought she was ready to change the status quo and create a new life for herself. She had no such plans, but the only way she could make him believe that was to end things with Cody.

She hurt all over, both for herself and for Cody. He didn't deserve this abrupt goodbye. He'd anticipated several more days of fun and games, but now he'd find out it was over. He'd treated her like a queen and this was a terrible way to repay him.

But she had no choice. She could only pray that he'd understand and not hate her forever. She would have continued their bargain if she could have and she'd do her best to explain that. He could still take Bert. Under the circumstances he might refuse, but she hoped not. A reliable horse was critical for an expedition like this and she wanted Cody to have the best.

Parking beside his truck, she walked down to the barn. Zane's truck was there. As she approached, she heard Zane and Cody joking around as they fed the horses.

She walked into the barn and was relieved that they were almost finished. They must have started super early to be this far along. "Hey, Zane," she called out. "If you have raptor cages to clean, I'll take it from here."

He tossed the hay flake he'd been holding back into the wheelbarrow. "Your headache gone?"

"Sure is."

"Then I'll accept that generous offer. Kyle's coming by first thing to examine a falcon with a broken wing. I'd like to be there."

She smiled at him. "Then take off, cowboy. I've got this."

"Thanks, Faith." He squeezed her shoulder as he walked past. "You're the best. See you guys later." Touching two fingers to the brim of his hat, he left the barn, moving fast.

Cody nudged back his hat and gazed at her. "I was hoping to see you this morning. Believe it or not, some idiot wants to show me his trailer at seven-thirty, so the minute I'm done here I have to take off."

She pulled on her gloves. "Then we'd better get moving."

"Not so fast, pretty lady." He rounded the wheelbarrow and came toward her. "I can always text him and tell him I'll be a few minutes late."

She drank in the sight of his strong, lean body. He'd worn a deep blue Western shirt that matched the color of his eyes. While he was delivering hay, he'd rolled back the sleeves to free up his forearms.

She noticed the pattern of dark hair sprinkled over them and wished she'd paid more attention when she'd had the chance. Would she remember how he looked without his shirt? Had she fully admired his strong thighs and muscular calves? If she hadn't, it was too late.

He pulled off his gloves and stuck them in his back pocket. "Got a kiss for me?"

She placed a restraining hand on his warm chest. "Let's finish feeding. Then we need to talk."

"I don't like the sound of that. Or the way you're looking at me. Is this bad news? Because if it is, give it to me, now."

Adrenaline pumped through her, making her heart hammer against her ribs. "My dad suspects that we're involved."

He took a deep breath. "To tell you the truth, that doesn't surprise me."

"He doesn't know everything, but for us to keep this up, I'd have to out-and-out lie to him. I can't do that."

He frowned. "What are you saying?"

"That it's over. We have to stop seeing each other." The depth of pain in his eyes was like a punch in the stomach. She'd expected him to be upset but not devastated.

His voice was thick with emotion. "You can't mean that."

"I do. He's ready to change everything by getting involved with Deidre. That's because he thinks I'm going to take up with you, or if not you, then someone else who might come along. I need to prove that I'm not going anywhere, which means it's the end for us. If I keep seeing you, he'll sense it."

"Don't do this. There has to be another way."

"There isn't." Her throat tightened. "I'm sorry, Cody. Do you want me to help you finish up here?"

"No. I want you to rethink your decision."

"I won't. Maybe I should just go." She turned and started back down the barn aisle.

"Wait." He caught her arm. "Before you leave, I have something to say."

17

Cody had been in tight spots before, but nothing like this. What he said in the next few minutes was so important. He hoped to hell he could say it right.

How ironic that Faith had chosen this moment to end it. He'd planned to have a talk with her tonight after they'd made love. He'd hoped to convince her they had a shot.

She stood very still, her green eyes filled with misery. She didn't want this breakup any more than he did, but she believed it was the only way to keep the dominoes from falling. He had some thoughts about that, but he had to tread carefully.

He grasped her shoulders and she trembled. "Don't worry. I'm not going to try and persuade you with a kiss. I don't think that would work, and what I need to say is more important than kissing."

"It's no use, Cody." Her voice was clogged with emotion. "I hate that we have to stop seeing each other, but that time would have come soon, anyway."

"It wouldn't have to."

"Yes, it would. There's no way it would work out for us."

He took a deep breath and let it out slowly. "I disagree. To start with, we could end the secrecy. I'm proud to tell the world that we're together. I think everyone would be happy for us."

"Not necessarily. My dad—"

"He likes me. I could talk with him. I'd reassure him that I'd never mess with the relationship he has with you. I'm not a threat." He smiled. "I might even be an asset."

"You don't live here."

"No, but you do. That's a powerful reason to relocate."

Her eyes widened. "You'd quit your job?"

"Yes, ma'am."

"But Kendra says it's a great guest ranch and you like it there. She said your boss is wonderful. He gave you time off for your trip during the busy summer season, which was very generous."

"That's all true." He held her gaze and gently massaged her shoulders. "It's the perfect job for a young, unattached guy who wants to get away from home so he can figure out what he wants. That used to be me. It's not anymore."

She shook her head. "You're talking crazy. You can't just go quitting a perfectly good job because—"

"Faith, I want to be with you. I want to give us a chance to see where this is going. I can't do that living three hours away. I'll find something around here. Hell, I might talk Mom into expanding this operation, putting up another barn." He searched for a spark of hope, maybe even some excitement in her eyes.

Instead there was only anxiety. "I can't believe this. You're ready to rip up your whole life, even change Kendra's life! What's next? Are you about to tell me you're canceling your trip, too?"

She wasn't reacting at all the way he'd hoped, but at least they were getting everything out in the open. It might take a while for her to move past her initial shock so that she could hear what he was saying. "I'm not canceling my trip."

"Thank God for that. You were really starting to worry me with this talk of quitting your job and doubling the size of Wild Creek's operation."

"I don't have to take the trip now, though. I can postpone it until next summer."

"*What?*" She stared at him. "You're kidding me, right?"

"Nope. It makes sense. By next summer Mom will be fully recovered. Whatever job I get will be with the understanding I'm taking those two months off. Best of all, I'm sure we could work it out with Mom and Zane so you can go with me. I found this awesome silver trailer that's a double, and if it's still available—"

"Stop!" Her expression had gone from anxious to full-blown panic. She backed away from him, breathing hard. "Stop talking about putting it off. That was never part of the plan. You have to take that trip *now*."

"No, I don't. I realized that last night while I was lying awake trying to figure this out. Faith, I want you to go, too. You would love it. I would love having you with me."

"I'm not going with you because you're taking your trip this summer. You've been planning this for *years*. And now, just because I wanted to find out what sex was like—"

"Not sex. Making love."

"I don't care what you call it, you're not giving up your dream because of it or because of me! I'd never forgive myself."

"But can't you see?" He took a step toward her, hand outstretched. "This is what I want to do, what I choose to do, and if you'll allow yourself time to think about it, you'll know it's right."

"It's not right." She was shaking. "If I had known that asking you for this favor would make you consider giving up your dream..." She gulped. "I never would have asked."

Pain sliced through him. "You regret what we've had?"

"You bet I do."

"Please don't say that." All that joy, down the drain? He couldn't stand it. "We've been good for each other. I know we have."

"Have we? Before I came along, you were totally focused on this quest. You should hear how Kendra talks about you, how proud she is of your dedication. I will *not* be the reason you give up on something so precious. You need to leave. The sooner, the better!" Turning, she ran out of the barn.

When she came back a second later, his heart filled with hope. He started toward her, ready to scoop her up in his arms if she gave the slightest indication she regretted her hasty exit. He was a romantic, after all.

But she didn't move in his direction, which was a bad sign. She gulped for air. "I still want you to take Bert." Then she turned around and left.

He had no idea how long he stood waiting, praying she'd come back again, ready to talk some more. Even if they only discussed the logistics of him picking up the horse, it would be something to build on. But she didn't come back. Gradually hope drained away and pain flowed in to take its place. He ached all over, as if he had the flu.

If Winston, the barn's most talkative horse, hadn't let out a shrill whinny, no telling when he would have returned to his chore and delivered the last few hay flakes. Winston's bugle call reminded him that regardless of human drama, the animals had to be fed.

Oh, and he had an appointment to look at a trailer. He was going to be late, so he'd text the guy. But if the trailer was halfway decent, he'd buy it. Might as well.

* * *

The trailer turned out to be in good shape and the price wasn't bad. It was green instead of silver and wouldn't go with the truck very well. Cody didn't care anymore. He paid for it and left it with the guy so he could stop by the grocery store and pick up the non-perishables he'd need for the trip.

He wasn't in any hurry to get back to the ranch, so he consulted the list of supplies he carried in his wallet to see what else he was missing. Not much.

A few more small camping items, a trip to the department store for extra briefs and socks, and he was done. After grabbing a burger for lunch, he put air in the tires and bought several cans of oil at George's Garage. If he did laundry tonight, he'd be ready to leave whenever he wanted.

Yeah, well, he didn't want to leave. Once he drove away, that would be it. On the other hand, staying at the ranch with nothing much to do except work around the barn was a bad idea. He'd run into Faith all the time. Or was that a good idea? Maybe if he stayed long enough, she'd come to her senses.

Rolling that thought around in his mind, he picked up the trailer and headed back to the ranch. It was only mid-afternoon, so he was surprised to see Faith's antique Ford on the road headed back to town. Maybe she was running an errand for his mom.

The speed limit was thirty-five on this stretch, so he could see her clearly as they approached each other. Just glimpsing her through a windshield made his heart thud painfully. He lifted a finger off the wheel in the time-honored way cowhands greeted each other on the road. She didn't respond in kind, although she looked at him. Then she glanced at the trailer he was towing as she passed by.

He watched in his rearview mirror, willing her to make a U-turn. There wasn't much traffic and she could do it easy enough. But she didn't. Did she really wish he'd never made love to her? Or had she said that to emphasize her point?

Smacking the steering wheel with his fist, he allowed himself to cuss for a while. The hell of it was he couldn't talk to anyone about the situation. Neither could she. They were each caught in their own private hell.

He needed to get it together before he saw his mom, but he wondered if he'd be able to fool her. He'd never been able to before, and he was more upset now than he'd been in a long time. On the other hand, he'd be pulling in towing a new-to-him horse trailer. Maybe that would distract her.

She was sitting on the porch with Deidre when he drove up. That would help. It wasn't uncommon for Deidre to stop by during the day if she happened to be in the neighborhood. His mom's other friends had jobs that kept them glued to a desk, but Deidre was free to roam.

He could guess why she'd come today. She and his mom were likely doing a post mortem on the party. They might be discussing Jim, but they also might be speculating as to why he'd been so eager to take Faith home, especially considering her spectacular makeover.

Instead of parking in his usual spot, he pulled across in front of the walkway so they could get a good look at his rig without having to go so far. His mom made her way down the steps. Deidre stayed close but made no attempt to help.

His mom smiled as she hobbled toward him. "So you finally made a decision."

"It was a good deal."

"I know nothing about horse trailers," Deidre said, "but it sure is green."

"Are you going to leave it that color?" His mom gazed at him. "You were being so picky about your choice that I expected you to get one that went with your truck."

He shrugged. "Maybe if I keep it I'll repaint it. It'll do the job for now." He ignored the look his mom was giving him. Settling for something that didn't look right wasn't his usual style. But a nice paint job would take several days. If he'd still been stalling because of Faith, that would have been fine.

"By the way, Faith gave me a message for you before she went home."

Damn, even hearing her name jacked up his pulse rate. "She went home?"

"She needed to," Deidre said. "That headache she had last night must have meant she was coming down with something. She looked terrible."

"She did, poor thing." His mom shook her head. "Like she'd been run over by a truck. I told her to get some rest. We can manage without her if she needs to take a couple of days off."

"I'm sorry to hear she's under the weather." He doubted she had a bug but he hated that she felt so bad about the breakup that she'd had to make an excuse to his mom. "What was the message?"

"She was convinced you'd buy a trailer today. Don't know why she thought so since you've looked at so many without buying one. But she said if you bought a trailer, you could come over and get Bert."

She must really want him gone. "But she's sick. I shouldn't bother her when she's not feeling good."

"Jim will be there. He can help you load Bert."

"Oh. I suppose he could." Faith had set it up so she wouldn't have to be a part of it. Here he'd looked forward to fetching Bert because it would give him one more chance to talk with her. She'd nipped that in the bud. Time to get out of town. "Did she say what time she wanted me to come by?"

"Whenever it's convenient."

Cody glanced at his mom. "We don't have a spare stall. Wouldn't it be better if I got him on my way out of town?"

She gave him a soft smile. "Forgive me for being sentimental, but I want you to leave from here."

"You do?"

"This day has been a long time coming and I want to take a few pictures and wave goodbye knowing you're heading out, not simply driving over to Faith and Jim's house. We can double up a couple of our horses and make room for Bert. Besides, this way you can test out your trailer."

"That's a good point." Faith had been right. His mother was excited about his journey, more than he was at the moment. He didn't want to disappoint her, either. "But I hate to just show up over there. I should alert Jim. I don't have his number."

"I do." Deidre pulled out her phone.

"Uh, great." Cody took his from his pocket and entered the info Deidre reeled off. "Thanks."

"Tell him I said hello."

"I will." He moved away from his mom and Deidre before calling Jim.

When Jim answered, he sounded subdued. "Hey, Cody. Let me step out on the porch."

Cody grew alarmed. "Is Faith okay?" Maybe she was sick, after all.

"She claims to have caught some nasty bug, but I've nursed that girl through quite a few bouts of flu and I don't think that's the problem."

"What do you think it is?"

"She's upset because I showed an interest in Deidre. She thinks her world is going haywire and it's got her down. Cody, I swear to God I've stayed away from women all this time because I was afraid it would create a problem for her. But when she became friends with you, I thought...well, never mind what I thought. I just don't know what to do now."

If Cody wasn't mistaken, Jim was asking him for advice. He had none to give, but he couldn't make himself say that and leave the poor guy with nothing. "It's a tricky situation."

"You're telling me."

"By the way, I got your number from Deidre. She says hello."

"Say hello for me."

"I will. Listen, Jim, would now be a good time for me to come and get Bert? I finally bought a trailer."

"Sure, come on over. Do you have time for a beer?"

"Why not?" If he was cut off from Faith, he might as well make friends with her dad.

18

Barricaded in her room, Faith paced the floor and debated why doing the right thing had to be so awful. She had a knot in her stomach the size of a basketball.

When her dad's phone rang downstairs, she knew it had to be Cody asking about coming to get Bert. She'd set that up before leaving the ranch. After that she'd seen his trailer with her own eyes, so she'd been expecting him to respond to her message.

He would be coming here any time now. She'd know when he loaded up Bert because she could see the barn from her bedroom window, the same one where she'd stood naked that first night they'd had sex. No, the night they'd first made love. Remembering what they'd shared, she knew the truth—they'd made love every single time.

That was Cody's doing, because she hadn't yet understood. He'd been the one who'd brought candles to add some romance to her initiation. He'd insisted on camping mattresses in the clearing because he hadn't wanted her to end up bruised. When she'd requested wild and crazy up against the truck, he'd warned her about the cold metal and then he'd protected her from it, cradling her in his arms so that she'd felt only pleasure.

The last time they'd held each other, when he'd informed her that they'd officially graduated to making love, he'd treated her with such tenderness. He'd let her into his heart as she'd let him into hers. But she'd never expected that their emotional connection would sabotage his dreams.

She'd been unaware that she was playing with fire. Her reading should have warned her that a man inflamed with passion could make foolish choices, but surely Cody was stronger than that. She'd trusted his single-minded dedication to his goal and she'd seriously underestimated her power to influence his plans.

Cutting off all communication had caused them both terrible pain. But once he corrected his course, once he'd set out on this journey that he'd planned for so long, he'd be all right. Surely this suffering was for his own good. If it was worth nothing, she'd go crazy.

Her dad was worried about her and she hated that, but after Cody had left on his quest, she'd pull herself together and return to normal. That process would begin soon, because Cody was coming for her horse. She would count the minutes until he left with Bert.

She heard his truck and went to the window. The trailer wasn't what she'd expected. She'd envisioned something more elegant, more in keeping with his snazzy truck. This one was a nice shade of green but it didn't add a thing to his midnight blue truck with its silver pin-striping.

He might have grabbed the first sturdy trailer he found. She was sorry he hadn't ended up with one that fit his personality, but getting him on the road was more important and she'd pushed him to accomplish that.

Her dad walked around the house and Cody climbed out of the truck. He glanced up at her window and she stepped back, not wanting him to see her. He probably couldn't in this light but she didn't want to take chances.

He wore the same blue shirt from this morning but the sleeves were rolled down. She wrapped her arms around her middle, feeling as if she had to hold herself together or she'd fly apart from the pain of looking at him. He was so beautiful. So loving. Naturally he wanted to take her with him on his quest. That was Cody, wanting to share, willing to postpone his dream to give her something special.

Standing a safe distance back from the window, she watched the two men examining the trailer. They were about the same height although Cody was more solidly built. Her dad had always been on the lanky side. But they had a similar way of moving, a similar way of standing with their legs slightly bowed from years of riding. Anyone watching them would know they were cowboys.

Her dad gestured toward the far side of the house. Because Cody was hauling a trailer, he'd be better off going that way to get back on Wagon Wheel Lane instead of trying to execute a U-turn.

The preliminaries were handled. Next they'd go into the barn and fetch Bert. It was almost over.

But instead of going into the barn, her dad patted Cody on the shoulder and they walked back around the house. What the hell? The sound of the front door opening threw her into a panic.

The soft rumble of their voices told her they were both in the house. The refrigerator opened and closed. Then they went out the door again. When they didn't reappear down by the barn, she could only draw one conclusion. They were sitting on the porch having a beer. Shitfire.

* * *

Being this close to Faith without seeing her was driving Cody nuts. He should never have agreed to have a beer with Jim while Faith hid upstairs in her room. But his romantic little heart had hoped that if he hung out with her dad, she'd crack and come down.

And then what? He still didn't want to leave without her. He got the impression that if he insisted on postponing it, she'd lose all respect for him. His mom might not be too happy, either.

Best case scenario, she'd come down, declare her feelings and promise to be here when he came back. How could he leave if she did something like that? But he'd have to. Then he'd spend two long months missing her.

He might not have to worry about that because he was halfway through his beer and she hadn't shown up. He and Jim had swapped stories about horses they'd known, from the best to the worst. Jim sounded a little wistful talking about his cowboying days, but Cody wasn't about to open that can of worms and suggest he get back to doing what he loved.

"Son, let me ask you something." Instead of looking at Cody, Jim stared at the mountains and rested his beer bottle on his knee.

Cody recognized the body language of a man who wanted info but was a little uncomfortable asking for it. "Shoot."

"You've known Deidre a long time."

"All my life."

"Can you picture her hanging out with a guy like me?"

Cody should have seen it coming when Jim had asked him to stay for a beer. He'd wanted a man-to-man talk with someone who might know the answer to that question. If Faith had heard it she'd go ballistic, but he doubted she was inside with her ear to the front door.

Not that Cody had a decent answer for Jim. He stalled with a question. "Is that what you're hoping for?"

"I'll admit I am. I've started to see that Faith and I are in a rut. A nice rut, but too confining. When she made friends with you, she poked her head out a little. Scared herself, I think, but I'm hoping she'll get over it and realize it's time for a change. For both of us."

Cody swallowed. "That would be great."

"But she's dead set against any kind of permanent change. I think that includes me hanging out with Deidre."

"I can tell you what she told me."

Jim's startled glance met his. "She talked to you about this?"

"Yes, sir."

"Then you two are better friends than I thought. She doesn't open up to just anybody. What did she say?"

"Maybe it's not so much what she said, but what I read between the lines. She's terrified of somehow losing what you have together."

"My God." Jim scrubbed a hand over his face. "That's impossible. I would never let that happen."

"Then you're on the same page."

"Absolutely." He looked over at Cody. "But I can imagine some changes that might be positive ones. Like you. I wouldn't mind having you around more often. You're good for Faith."

Cody's breath caught. "I'm probably stepping way out of line, but I wish you'd tell her." Adrenaline pumped through him, making him shaky.

"I will tell her. And reassure her that I'd never let Deidre come between us, either."

"I think she's more worried about you getting hurt."

Jim gazed at him. "I've been hurt, son. Nothing hurts worse than having someone you love die, especially long before their time. I'm sure your mother knows that."

"I'm sure she does."

"Maybe I need to remind my daughter that I'm tougher than she thinks. I'm touched that she's worried about me, but if Deidre and I get together and she eventually kicks me to the curb, I can handle it. I'll just choose better next time."

"Sounds like a plan."

"What about you and Faith?"

Cody met his gaze. "I don't know, Jim. I care for her, but...I just don't know."

"I can tell she cares for you, too." He reached over and squeezed Cody's shoulder. "I'll talk to her. Now let's go load Bert."

* * *

At long last, Faith heard activity down at the barn. She looked out her window and watched her dad lead Bert out while Cody let down the ramp to the trailer. She'd miss her sweet horse and he'd miss her, but that was nothing compared to the gut-wrenching loss of not seeing Cody every day. He'd miss her, too. She hoped by the time he came back, he'd be over her.

She'd never be over him, but she'd have to figure out a way not to show it. She'd miscalculated on several things when she'd planned this episode. Her biggest mistake was not realizing how deep the connection would become in a few days.

She hadn't meant that to happen. Although the books had described brief affairs that created strong emotions, she'd assumed the authors were exaggerating for dramatic effect. As she gazed down at Cody helping her dad load Bert, she concluded the books hadn't gone far enough.

Cody shot the bolt on the trailer, locking Bert in. He shook hands with her dad and to her surprise gave him a quick hug. Tears blurred her vision and she wiped them away. She didn't want to miss a single thing.

He climbed behind the wheel of his truck, closed the door and rolled down the window. Leaning out, he continued to talk with her dad. Her dad nudged back his hat and rested his hand on the doorframe, almost as if he didn't want Cody to leave.

When Cody faced forward and started the engine, her dad backed away. Cody put two fingers to the brim of his hat and her dad waved. Slowly the truck moved and then picked up a little speed. Her dad stood where he was until both truck and trailer were out of sight.

Faith didn't realize she was crying until a sob nearly choked the life out of her. Flinging herself on her bed, she buried her face in her pillow and beat her fists on the mattress. She'd never cried like this, never. And she hated it.

Gradually the noisy sobs diminished enough that the sound of her father calling her name and tapping on her door penetrated her fog. She had no idea how much time had passed. Dinner might be ready, although she didn't smell cooked food.

She did her best to clear her throat. "Not hungry, Dad."

"I need to talk to you."

"Maybe later, okay?"

"Now."

She sat up. She hadn't heard him use that tone since the time she'd decided to ride a very green horse when she was ten. He'd given her a long lecture that day. Maybe he was planning to give her one now. She probably deserved it.

Grabbing a tissue, she blew her nose, but there was no fixing the rest of her. She was a mess. "You can come in."

He entered and his jaw dropped. "Oh, honey bun."

That started the water works all over again. She snatched up her pillow and pressed it to her face while she tried to get control of herself.

The mattress dipped and her dad's arm came around her shoulders. "You're in love with him."

She kept crying, but she nodded.

"For what it's worth, he's in love with you, too."

She nodded again.

"He said you're worried about me."

Rubbing the soggy pillow over her face, she put it on her lap and blinked away tears as she gazed into his dear face. "I am."

His grip on her shoulders tightened. "About Deidre?"

She nodded.

He handed her his red bandanna. "I like her. I think we could have fun together, but it doesn't mean what you and I have will change. We're a team." He gave her a squeeze. "We'll always be a team, no matter who else comes into our lives."

She blew her nose on his bandanna and wiped her eyes. Then she laid her head on his shoulder. "I've been kind of an idiot, haven't I?"

"People sometimes act like idiots when they're in love. They get funny ideas about how things are or how they should be. They don't always think straight. But I'll tell you this, that's one fine young man. If you let him get away, then you'll be an even bigger idiot."

She lifted her head and scooted away so she could see his face. "What am I supposed to do? He's leaving. For all I know, he's leaving tonight."

"No, tomorrow. You still have time to go over there and tell him how you feel."

"I can't. If I do, then he'll start talking about postponing his trip and we'll be right back where we started."

"What do you mean, postpone it?"

She combed her hair back from her damp cheeks. "He asked me to go, but that means putting it off until next summer. He can't do that, Dad! It's his dream that he's planned since he was in high school!"

"Why can't you go with him now?"

"Because I'm needed here! Kendra needs me. I agreed to this job and I—"

"Then maybe you should let Cody postpone his trip."

"No. Never." She looked him in the eye. "I refuse to be the reason he doesn't leave tomorrow."

"Even if that would be his choice?"

"You said it yourself. People in love aren't thinking straight. He has everything ready and he has the momentum. If he puts it off there's always a chance he'll never do it."

"I hate to admit it, but you have a point." He gave her shoulder another squeeze. "Will you be okay for a while if I go run a quick errand?"

"What errand?"

"Just something I need to do." He kissed her cheek. "Take a nice shower. That always makes a person feel better."

"I will. And thanks, Dad. Just talking it out with you has been huge."

"Good." He started toward the door.

"You're not going to tell me what this errand is, are you?"

"Not yet. Go take your shower."

Climbing out of bed, she walked to the bathroom. A shower would feel good. Telling her dad about Cody had felt good, too. Somehow she'd get through the next twelve hours and then Cody would be off on his adventure. That had to happen, no matter what.

19

Cody arrived back at the ranch to find Deidre gone but Zane, Mandy and Aunt Jo were there to have dinner. They all came down to the barn to admire the trailer and Zane helped Cody unload Bert and put him in the stall they'd made ready for him.

"He's a fine-looking horse." Zane patted Bert's sleek coat. "You two should get along great."

"We will." Cody couldn't look at Bert without thinking of Faith, though, and he hoped that wouldn't go on for two months. Everybody had asked about her since she was supposed to be sick. He'd confirmed that she must be feeling crappy since she'd stayed in her room the whole time he was there.

As they all walked back to the house, Mandy offered to come over and help the next day since Faith might not feel up to working yet.

Cody liked that plan. "Good idea. If she pushes herself, she might get worse." If he knew she wouldn't show up in the morning, he wouldn't have to bust a gut to leave before she arrived. He'd given up on some last-minute miracle. She wasn't going to make a dramatic gesture, no matter how much he wished she would.

But just as they reached the house and started up the steps to the porch, he heard a truck coming. He turned and nearly had a heart attack when he saw Faith's antique Ford pulling in.

"Maybe she's feeling better, after all," Mandy said.

Cody couldn't speak. His throat tight with anxiety, he stared at the truck. Then he saw who was driving. "It's Jim. He's alone." His first, irrational thought was that something was seriously wrong with Faith. But that made no sense. Jim wouldn't drive over here in that case. He'd call 911.

Zane glanced at Cody. "Maybe he forgot to tell you something about Bert."

"Maybe. Except he could've called me." Nobody had gone into the house. They must be as curious as he was about this unexpected visit.

Jim smiled as he approached. "This is lucky. You're all here. I was afraid you'd have to call a family meeting, but I see that won't be necessary."

Cody's mom was the first to speak. "What's up, Jim?"

"I'd like to apply for a job."

"A job?" She blinked. "Doing what?"

"Whatever Faith's been doing—working in the barn, guiding trail rides. I'm even a fair hand in the kitchen if you need me there."

Cody had trouble breathing. "Faith's not coming back?"

"Eventually I'm sure she'll want to." Jim looked at him. "But I figured if I filled in for a couple of months, that might work out for you."

Cody's ears buzzed. He hoped to hell he wasn't dreaming this conversation. "But I thought you were done with all that."

"I found a good reason to get back into it. I also realized that I'd stopped riding because I was worried about something happening to me that would leave Faith all alone." His gaze was steady as he trained it on Cody. "But she wouldn't be."

"Not if I can help it."

"I figured. Besides, I was getting bored. And this is what I know."

Zane scratched the back of his neck. "I'm so lost."

"I'm not." Mandy looked over at Cody. "I've worked with Faith for a couple of months and she never worried about how she looked. Then you show up and suddenly I'm altering her clothes. And you're jumping up to give her a ride home when she gets a headache."

Cody glanced at Aunt Jo, who was hiding a smile. She'd likely figured this out after their chance meeting at Pills and Pop, but hadn't said anything to Mandy.

"Oh!" His mom spun toward him. "The light dawns!" She smacked her forehead. "I can't believe I didn't pick up on it. But why keep it a secret?"

Cody sent Aunt Jo a look of gratitude. She hadn't told her best friend, either. "Faith asked me to."

"Why?" Then his mom waved her hand. "Never mind. I get it. She might have thought I wouldn't approve because she's an employee. But I still don't understand why Jim wants to take over her job."

Cody dragged in a breath. "I'd like her to go with me. But as long as she's needed here, she can't even consider that possibility."

"Oh. She's not really sick, is she?"

He shook his head.

"Heartsick," Mandy said.

"Well, that can be just as bad. And Cody, you haven't been yourself today, either. I thought you might be coming down with the same thing Faith had."

Mandy chuckled. "Which he was."

"My poor son." His mom hobbled over to him and took his face in both hands. "If I'd known, I would have found a way to let her go with you." A tender light shone in her eyes.

"She never would have stood for that. But I'm hoping she'll go for Jim's idea."

"Except I haven't landed the job yet," Jim said.

Cody's mom turned around to face him. "How are you at picking wildflowers?"

"Well, now, Kendra, I haven't picked wildflowers in a long, long time." His expression softened. "I used to do it for my wife. I reckon you don't forget how."

"You don't." There was a slight tremor in her voice. Then she glanced over at Zane. "Any objections if we hire this cowboy?"

Zane grinned. "No, ma'am. You won't catch me standing in the way of true love."

Cody had a sudden thought. He glanced at Jim. "Does Faith know what you're up to?"

"No." He held out the keys to the antique Ford. "But I figure you're the one to tell her and unhitching that trailer will take too long."

Cody's attention swerved from the keys dangling in Jim's hand to the trailer attached to his truck. "I bought the wrong damn trailer."

"It's a decent looking rig." Jim smiled at him. "I've been thinking I could use one if you're considering selling it."

"I am. We'll talk." He took the keys. "Thanks."

Jim waved a hand. "No problem. Go see my daughter and tell her there's been a change in plans. Then if you wouldn't mind bringing her back here, we can work out the details."

"Wait a minute," Mandy said. "Shouldn't they have some time alone?"

Jim's face turned red and he cleared his throat. "Uh, I didn't think of that."

"Don't think about it." Cody glanced around at the assembled group. "I guarantee Faith wouldn't want you to. Let's not embarrass her, okay? I'll bring her back and we'll work out the details, like Jim said."

"Hey, bro," Zane said, "you don't have to come *right* back. Mandy has a point."

"If Faith goes for this plan, we'll have plenty of time to be alone. Two whole months. See you soon." He hurried over to the truck.

He did his best not to break any speed limits on the way through town but he might've been a bit over. His foot just kept wanting to press harder on the pedal. God, he hoped Faith would agree to this. Her dad seemed to think it was a slam dunk but he wasn't so sure.

Faith was very protective of her father. She'd never allow him to sacrifice his safety and well-being for her needs. If she thought he was doing that, she'd turn thumbs down. As he'd learned, once she made up her mind about something, she couldn't be budged.

When he pulled up in front of the little frame house, the lights were on downstairs and he could smell something cooking, maybe chicken. He had a flash of what it would be like to come home to a house like this, to know that he would hold Faith in his arms at night and wake up with her in the morning. He wanted that. But first he had to convince her to make this trip.

As he walked toward the front porch, she came out the front door. "Okay, Dad, you'd better tell me..." She came to an abrupt halt. "What are you doing here? Where's my dad?"

"At the ranch." He mounted the steps. "He loaned me the truck so I could come and see you."

"I don't want to see you." But her eyes sent a different message and she was breathing fast. "Why's my dad at the ranch?"

"He applied for your job. He got it."

"You're not making any sense. Have you been drinking?"

"Not a drop." But he was feeling a little drunk standing so close he could smell soap, shampoo, and warm woman. She had on her normal baggy clothes and she'd put her hair in a braid, like usual. He'd never wanted to hold someone as much as he wanted to hold her. "Can I come in?"

"Why?"

"We have things to discuss." She'd left the door standing open and the aroma of chicken was stronger. "Are you fixing dinner?"

"I was expecting my dad. Cody, what's going on?"

"Let me come in and I'll explain. Give me five minutes."

"Okay, five minutes." She turned and went inside.

As he followed and closed the door behind him, he fought the urge to reach for her. She'd given him five minutes to lay out the new plan. He needed to make it concise and persuasive.

He took a deep breath, but the words that came out had nothing to do with the plan. "I love you."

Her green eyes filled with anguish. "Cody, if you've come here to try and convince me that postponing your trip is a good idea, then you're wasting your time."

"No, that's not it. Did you hear what I said about your dad? He's been hired in your place."

"That's crazy! He's sworn off riding. He can't do my job. Why is he replacing me? Did I do something wrong?"

He was making a mess of this. "He wants to replace you for two months so you can go with me."

Her eyes widened. "What?"

"He wants us to go together. More than that, he wants us to *be* together. He came to the ranch just now and asked for a job. He's been hired."

"Was this your idea?"

"No! I had nothing to do with it, I swear."

"Just a minute. Let me turn off the stove." She stomped out of the living room. In seconds, she was back. "Let's go."

"Where?"

"To the ranch. I want to get to the bottom of this. Oh, and give me the keys. I'll drive."

He didn't have a choice. It was her truck. He'd promised everyone they'd be back soon, but he didn't think they were prepared for Faith on the warpath.

Once they got on the road, she started in. "Let me get this straight. When my dad left here, he drove to the ranch and asked if he could have my job so I could leave with you."

"That's about the size of it."

"Yet the other night he announced to you that he wasn't willing to risk his neck by climbing on the back of a horse."

"That was before he realized your job was standing in the way of going with me on this trip."

"So now he'll risk his neck so I can go traipsing around the countryside with you? I don't think so!"

He wanted to diffuse this bomb, but he wasn't sure how. "He said something that might interest you."

"What was that?"

"I take it he almost died after the horse rolled on him."

She was quiet for a moment. "Yes."

"Tonight he said he'd quit riding because he'd been afraid he'd die and leave you alone."

The cab of the truck was silent except for the hum of the tires. "I didn't know that," she said at last.

"If you don't believe me, you can ask him."

"I believe you. That sounds like my dad. He convinced me he was afraid for himself, but instead he was afraid for me."

"That's what he said."

"So why change his mind about that, now?"

He'd been so hoping she'd ask. "Two reasons. He's bored."

"I'm sure he is. What was his second reason?"

"He knows if something happens to him, you won't be alone." In the silence that followed, he could almost hear her thinking. He decided to press on. "He's right. You have us McGavins, now. But more than that, you have me."

"Cody, I—"

"I know you're having trouble believing that I love you. You may even think it's just sex."

"It could be, you know."

"But it's not. I know the difference. When you smile, I see the freckles across your nose and that little space between your front teeth and my heart melts. When you're all fixed up like you were last night, you're dynamite, but you don't need any of that to bring me to my knees. I love the Faith I first met, the one who dabbed vanilla on herself to convince me she was desirable."

She groaned. "I realize now that was so—"

"Adorable. Vanilla is now my favorite scent because it makes me think of you. Please consider accepting your father's generous gesture as it was meant."

"It was high-handed."

"It was loving."

"But is he up to the job?"

"Absolutely. He might need a week or two to get back in the swing of things, but he's been wrangling horses all his life. You know yourself he couldn't ask for a more nurturing environment than Wild Creek Ranch."

"No," she said softly. "He couldn't."

"Say you'll take this adventure with me, Faith. I'll buy that double trailer and we'll head into the unknown, plus your dad will have a second chance to do the work he loves."

"And get frisky with Deidre."

"Maybe, but he's up to the challenge."

"I didn't think so before, but a guy who'll drive right up to a ranch house and ask for a job out of the blue won't be intimidated by Deidre."

"No." Hope gave him a nudge, telling him not to give up. "Come with me, Faith."

"I'm scheduled to give Deidre riding lessons."

"Let your dad do it."

She laughed. "That would make a great YouTube video."

"I love you." He decided it might be time to remind her.

She swung the truck to the side of the road and killed the engine. "You keep saying that."

"Does it bother you?"

"No." She looked over at him, her face in shadows. "I like it."

"Good, because I like saying it." He hesitated, afraid to push, but she had pulled over. "Anything you care to say to me?"

"You're fishing."

"Yes, ma'am."

The click of her seatbelt disengaging was loud in the stillness of the cab. "I'm coming over."

"Over here?" Then suddenly he had a lapful of Faith. His hat got knocked somewhere and she was kissing him as if she couldn't get enough.

Breathing hard, she eased away from him. "I love you, too, but you've always known that."

"Not at first." He cupped the back of her head and drew her closer. "I thought I was the means to an end."

"That, too."

He smiled against her warm lips. "Thought so."

She lifted her head. "But I fell for you that first day. You were my fantasy, the only one for me."

"If I were a better man, I'd deny that I'm the best you'll ever find. But I'm not that noble. Stay with me, sweet lady. No one could ever love you more." In a world of uncertainties, he knew that much to be true. As he kissed her, he laid claim to a future filled with as much happiness as two hearts could hold. After all, he had Faith.

Sparks fly when Ryker McGavin crosses paths with his first love, April Harris, in A COWBOY'S RETURN, book three in the McGavin Brothers series!

* * * * *

April hadn't cuddled many newborns but this cherub seemed to fit in her arms just fine. She focused on the baby's unblinking stare. "Hello, little one." Blue eyes, but they might not stay blue. John's were hazel and her sister Leigh's were brown like April's. The little girl's hair was the color of wheat, but that could change, too.

John had her swaddled in a soft blanket but she'd worked one impossibly tiny hand out of the folds. "You are so precious." April offered her little finger and the baby gripped it. "You're one lucky girl, you know that?"

"I'll bet she does."

She glanced up at the sound of Ryker's voice and discovered he'd moved closer. "Want to hold her?"

"Oh, no." He took a step back. "She's brand new. I could louse it up."

"No, you can't. I'll be right here. Have you ever held a newborn?"

"Never. I can't remember the last time I held a baby, let alone one only hours old." Yet he seemed fascinated by the tiny girl.

"Then take this chance to experience it." She closed the short distance between them. "As big as you are, you'll only need one arm."

"April, I'm not—"

"Try it. You might like it." She slowly transferred the baby to him.

"Stay right here so nothing bad happens." He accepted the tiny girl with reluctance but he did take her.

"Nothing bad will happen. Isn't she sweet?"

He stood very still, his breathing unsteady as he cradled the baby in his arms and looked down at her, his expression dazed. "There's nothing to her. She's...like a baby bird."

"She is, a little bit, with her hair sticking up like that." Her voice wavered and she hoped he wouldn't notice.

She'd made a mistake encouraging him to hold this child. The image of him clutching a tiny baby to his massive chest would haunt her. She'd imagined it so many times when she'd been desperately in love with him. Now here he was standing before her, the embodiment of her teenage fantasies. But the baby wasn't theirs.

New York Times bestselling author Vicki Lewis Thompson's love affair with cowboys started with the Lone Ranger, continued through Maverick, and took a turn south of the border with Zorro. She views cowboys as the Western version of knights in shining armor, rugged men who value honor, honesty and hard work. Fortunately for her, she lives in the Arizona desert, where broad-shouldered, lean-hipped cowboys abound. Blessed with such an abundance of inspiration, she only hopes that she can do them justice.

For more information about this prolific author, visit her website and sign up for her newsletter. She loves connecting with readers.

VickiLewisThompson.com

CPSIA information can be obtained
at www.ICGtesting.com
Printed in the USA
BVHW032213081118
532372BV00030B/298/P

781946 759146